PERFECT

ITALIAN LOVERS, BOOK 1

DIANA FRASER

Perfect
(also published as The Italian's Perfect Lover)
by Diana Fraser

© 2011 Diana Fraser

—Italian Lovers—
The Italian's Perfect Lover
Seduced by the Italian
The Passionate Italian
An Accidental Christmas

You can sign up to Diana's newsletter here (or via her website) for more information on book releases.

For more information about this author visit:
www.dianafraser.net

CHAPTER 1

*A*lessandro Cavour, Conte di Montecorvio Rovella, watched as the voluptuous blonde, who had just gate-crashed his party, popped a third piece of bruschetta into her mouth.

If she was trying to fit in she was going the wrong way about it. Women in his world barely ate; they wore only black—not a blood-red sheath—and curves were not an option.

"Shall I have her removed, sir?"

Alessandro shook his head and drank the last of his whisky, relishing its fire. He needed fire. He needed a diversion. And he'd just found one.

"No. Leave her to me."

Where was he?

Emily Carlyle brushed the crumbs from her dress and anxiously scanned the room for the elderly count upon whom all her hopes were pinned.

She needed to mingle. God, how did she do that?

1

She needed to fit in. And she certainly didn't do that.

Her hand rose to push her glasses more firmly on her nose before she remembered she'd left them off tonight. Not, she thought, peering around the room, that there had been any point.

She was surrounded by the cream of Neopolitan society: moneyed, elegant, perfect. And she was none of these things. And never would be.

She tugged the wrap more securely around her shoulders. She might not be ashamed of her imperfections but there was no reason to display them—not tonight—not when so much was riding on it.

Where the hell was he?

Suddenly she felt a chill of awareness slither down her spine: someone was watching her. She turned slowly to see a man—blurred a little at first—moving through the crowded room towards her, staring directly at her. When he came into focus she could see his coal-black eyes held both heat and cool control: predator's eyes.

Her heart pounded once, fiercely, before settling into a fast tattoo that sent adrenalin racing through her veins, stimulating her body into a state of readiness. Fight or flight? At that instant, she could do neither.

Then the crowd parted and the man emerged and stood before her. There was nothing about his appearance that contradicted her first instinct. A predator took whatever he wanted and she knew this man could do just that. It wasn't just that he was the most striking man she'd ever seen; it wasn't simply that he was the most charismatic—although conversations had stalled in his wake and all eyes were on him; it was his difference to the others that signaled his power.

In a room of immaculately dressed people, this man stood before her disheveled and arrogant. His black tie hung loosely either side of his open shirt and his hair—raked back as if by careless fingers—hung in tactile curls on his collar. He either didn't notice he was flouting convention or he didn't care. She'd bet her life it was the latter.

This was a man who was used to getting his own way; this was a man who didn't want to be here.

There, they had something in common.

She stepped back to move out of his way. Because she hadn't lived twenty-six years without knowing that men, that gorgeous, didn't make a bee-line for her.

But he also side-stepped so he stood squarely in front of her.

He looked even better close up. She was preternaturally aware of the textures on his face: a day's worth of stubble, the lines that bracketed his mouth and of an errant curl that fell like a question mark on his forehead.

She swallowed hard.

That men like this existed, she'd never imagined. That one could be touching her arm, with an intimacy that sent shivers down her spine, was impossible.

"Scusi."

"Sure, sorry," she mumbled, stepping aside so he could pass.

He smiled. "No, signorina. It is you I've come to speak with."

She could feel her eyes widen in shock and opened her mouth to reply only to find her voice had somehow diminished to a whisper.

"I think you've got the wrong woman."

"*Davvero?*"

Her eyes dropped to his lips: amusement flickered at their corners.

She nodded. "Really."

"And who would be the right woman?"

She shrugged. "Anyone else."

He frowned. "Your husband or boyfriend is here?"

"No, I don't have one."

"Ah, then you are free to talk."

Her irritation, at his presumption that a boyfriend would be the only reason why she wouldn't want to talk with him, should have brought her back to her senses.

"But I don't know you—"

"We can remedy that —"

"And I can't think why you would want to speak with me. Perhaps you've mistaken me for someone else?"

"I always make it a point to speak to the most beautiful woman in the room. And if I've mistaken you for such, then perhaps it is because you are."

The instinctive laugh froze on her lips. There was something about his manner, about his tone, about the expression in his eyes, which stopped her reacting with her usual self-deprecating humor.

She knew it to be a lie but *how* persuasive, *how* devastating, it was to hear such words addressed to her. She'd spent years avoiding her femininity, scared of being seen as an object. Bitter experience had taught her that objects could be owned and possessed and people did what they liked with their possessions, even tried to destroy them.

Now, she'd just walked straight into what she'd been avoiding all these years. And it thrilled her like nothing before.

He *was* like no-one before.

She took a deep breath in order to ground herself. "Thank you for the compliment."

His lips curved briefly into a smile that lingered in the lines around his mouth and in the flicker of heat in his eyes.

"You're not used to this, are you?"

His candor dispelled her nerves and, for the first time, she glanced away from him, trying to suppress a smile.

"Is it so obvious?"

"Obvious and refreshing."

"What gave me away? I guess it's the dress," she looked down frowning at the red dress. "Hardly the usual color, it would seem."

"You stand out. But it is not that alone."

"What then?" She grabbed the ends of the shawl to make sure they stayed in place and folded her arms across her breasts. "I guess I eat, which clearly sets me apart from the other women."

"It does." He leaned forward and whispered conspiratorially in her ear. "And a very good thing, too. But it is not that either."

"What then?"

"Your lack of awareness."

"Of?"

"People. My guess is that you don't attend many such parties."

"And you would know this because?"

He hesitated for one long second, enough for her to note the shading under his eyes and the stark lines of his cheek and jaw. The predator was hungry.

"Because you look and don't see; you don't notice the inquisitive stares, the jealous looks, the admiring glances. They don't affect you. I think you must live away from society—some kind of recluse, maybe?"

Emily could feel the blood drain out of her face. How could he tell? How could he know that her world, as an archaeologist, was the world of the past, where the only people who mattered had been dead for centuries?

"I am correct?"

She nodded, spellbound by this man who could see into her heart.

Part of her knew it to be the result of clever, well-honed flirtation skills, pick-up lines well learned, but the greater part of her didn't care. She felt a connection with him slide smoothly into place.

"How did you know?" Her voice, normally so strong and so confident, sounded cracked, fractured.

"By your lack of consciousness—in your body, but most of all in your eyes." He cocked his head to one side. "Green eyes."

She gasped down a lungful of air like a dying woman desperate for life and shook her head.

"Kind of more like blue-ish with yellow streaks—"

"You," he brushed her cheek with the back of his finger, "are too prosaic. Your eyes are green. Unusual. A dark green: the color of a pine forest in twilight, of wet, gold-streaked jade, the color of a secret. What, I wonder, is yours?"

Somehow the stranger had brought himself so close to her that she could smell his intoxicating blend of aftershave —earthy, warm and very, very male—and whisky. Impercep-tibly—surely he would hardly notice—she dipped her head towards his neck and inhaled his more personal scent. She swallowed and looked away as she felt the heat fire deep inside her, stirring something she'd thought long dead, never to be revived.

His own face inclined to hers briefly in response. The feel of his hair grazing her cheek made her jump back in alarm.

Suddenly music flooded the room. A small quartet, making a very large sound, made further conversation impossible.

"Come."

She balked for an instant at his imperious command. But

then he ran his fingers down her shawl-covered arm until he held her hand, and all resistance fled.

"Let's escape." He nodded towards the open French windows.

As he pulled her outside, the sultry stir of the evening breeze awakened Emily from the haze of lust this man stirred.

She hesitated, and stopped abruptly. What was she doing?

"I should go—go back inside. I need to, well, go."

He turned to face her. "So soon?"

"It should have been sooner. I'm not in the habit of wandering around in the dark with strangers. I don't even know your name."

He smiled. "My name is Alex."

"And mine, Em."

"M? That is an unusual name." He raised an eyebrow. "Not the 'M' from James Bond, not the secret head of MI5?"

She grinned, relaxing, the tension falling away. "No, not."

"Perhaps short for Miranda, or Miriam?"

"Perhaps."

"So cagey. That is fine. I will call you M. So, M, why are you here?"

She suddenly realized why this beautiful man was talking to her, why he'd taken her away from the party she'd gate-crashed. He was very smoothly ejecting her. She'd thought he was flirting with her. She'd thought wrong.

Disappointment bit deep. She'd tried hard to fit in, had made a massive leap outside her comfort zone, borrowing a dress and too-tight shoes, but had still failed. But there was too much riding on it. She needed to see the count, even if it meant bluffing her way back inside.

"What makes you think I haven't been invited?"

He dipped his head, uncomfortably close to hers.

"*Cara*," his breath tickled her skin, halting her own

breathing. "I know you haven't. It's my party and I know everyone here, except you."

His words cut like ice, severing her last remaining thread of hope.

He had no interest in her. And he'd effectively killed her work stone dead because if she couldn't see the count, she had nothing. Without the count's financial support her work would have to end.

"I'm sorry. I'll go. I was just—looking for someone. I'd been told he was here. But he's not. So—"

"You misunderstand me. I do not wish you to go."

"I shouldn't be here."

She looked up at him, at this knowing man who'd broken through her defenses after all these years, willing him to contradict her.

He smiled, as if recognizing the token comment for what it was.

"And neither should I, believe me. I should be at the party, but I have never been interested in duty. It is pleasure that interests me."

"I can see that."

"Come," he offered his arm, "let's leave the party before someone either turns you away, or worse still, forces me to do my duty and make small talk."

She laughed. "Somehow, I can't imagine anyone forcing you to do anything." And then she hesitated.

Thoughts of caution flashed through her mind, fighting the instincts and needs of her body.

But her body won and she inhaled the fragrant night air and took his arm.

Spring flowers tumbled around the stone-flagged pathway along which they walked, but Emily was only aware of the silk of his jacket and the heat of his arm under her fingertips.

Within moments, she found herself seated in a secluded courtyard, enclosed by a high yew hedge, in the centre of which a small fountain played. Moon-white flowers clustered at its base.

"So, M, relax and tell me about yourself."

"Nothing much to tell." She could barely breathe, let alone think, with his body in such close proximity.

He turned towards her, his arm resting along the back of the seat, close to her shoulders. Her skin prickled, as if her body responded to his magnetism by the force of physics alone. And she knew all about the inevitability of the laws of science. But how they applied here was beyond her education.

"So, where have you been hiding, M, that you are so unused to people? So unaware of your effect on my guests?"

"What effect could I possibly have?"

He searched her eyes before shaking his head. "You have no idea, do you? No idea how very different you are."

Different? Another thing they had in common.

Heat swept through her body, following the path of his eyes. "English, I look English." She said hopefully.

"It is not that. You look," his hand brushed down her arm lightly before resting once more on the seat, "sensual, very sensual."

She tensed then. She wasn't used to being touched. But his eyes held only interest—a wonderful, inexplicable interest that her body exulted in—and gentleness. This wasn't a man like her last—her only—boyfriend. There was no rage there, no insecurity, no jealousy, no violence. She exhaled jaggedly.

History could repeat itself—as an archaeologist she knew that—but it didn't have to, not if she learned from the lessons of the past. She'd never trusted her intuition before—not even when it screamed at her to run from her ex-boyfriend—but now she did.

"Sensual?" No-one had ever said such a thing before. But she felt sensual. The skimming fit of the borrowed dress against her body, rubbing her skin, tantalized her arousal even further, the warmth of the night breeze on her skin. And this man.

"Of the senses."

"Such as sight?" Hesitantly at first, she allowed her gaze to travel from his hair, curling where he'd pushed it roughly back, to the pulse that thudded in his neck and then down to his chest and legs before resting once more on his face.

"Sight is indeed a sense." His voice was roughened, deeper somehow.

Her effect on him gave her a sense of power. She closed her eyes.

"And sound." The soft exhalation of his breath was louder to her than the rustle of the leaves high above them and the distant music and laughter. She opened her eyes again. "What else? Touch?"

Dare she? If he'd moved she would have retreated, but he didn't. He said nothing but she could see his eyes narrow and darken as she reached out to his arm, pausing only briefly before touching the sleeve of his black tux. The tentative touch turned into an appreciative slide of her finger tips—more used to dirt and rough rocks—across the dense silk.

She knew she should stop but felt compelled to continue. "Such as," she leaned into his neck, "smell".

His breathing quickened against her face. She couldn't see now because she'd closed her eyes, all the better to register the different notes of his aftershave, the spring air against his skin and a deeper note, that her mind couldn't identify, but to which her body reacted.

Reluctantly she sat back. "What else?"

"You tell me." He didn't move, simply looked at her lips as if anticipating something delicious, something he wasn't going to take unless it was offered. The predator might be hungry, but he was patient.

All thought of who she was, of where she was, of her past, disappeared. There was nothing except this man.

"Taste."

She didn't move. She was sure she didn't move. But somehow their faces were so close that their mouths were a mere whisper apart.

She wanted him to kiss her but no kiss came. Instead she felt his hand touch her cheek, gently, so gently that she couldn't have said whether it was him or the soft breeze. It was a tender, lingering exploration: stimulating, rather than controlling. This wasn't a man who needed to prove anything; this was a man who wanted to experience everything.

He pulled away slightly as if to question her, his hand still barely touching her cheek, his fingertips tracing the curve of her cheekbone. Whatever expression she had in her eyes seemed to have given him an answer because he dipped his head and held it close to hers for one long moment—lips not touching, his cheek brushing hers.

She'd never known the exquisite tensions that now flowed through her body; never felt the gentle touch of a lover's hand; had never felt so in tune with another that her mind became suspended and her body took over.

For one delicious moment she surrendered to his touch that stimulated every nerve ending in her body; for one intense second, the world forgot to breathe and she held herself in that moment, only with him, *feeling* through him; for one instant she felt perfect.

But she wasn't perfect, was she?

"No." She pulled away from him, overwhelmed by the

grief-filled knowledge that she could never be this man's lover.

The blind darkness of his lust-filled eyes lightened with confusion. "I am sorry. Forgive me." He blinked, as if awaking from a daze, and rose abruptly.

Like her attraction, she felt his withdrawal as a physical sensation, a pain that made her flex her hands for relief. "It's me who should apologize. I practically forced myself on you."

He smiled. "Believe me, our attraction proved mutually strong." His smiled faded into a frown as if he couldn't understand the reason why.

She turned away from him then. No, of course he wouldn't know why. Why would he, a devastatingly handsome man be attracted to her, Emily Carlyle from East London: an academic, a spinster and most definitely *not* the most beautiful woman at the party?

He reached out to her tentatively, as if to reassure—either her or himself—before he thrust both hands back into his pockets.

"Come, I will take you back."

Of course he would.

He had no interest in her. Why would he? There was a room full of beautiful women awaiting his pleasure. His responses to her were automatic—the result of a lust-filled woman, wearing very little, throwing herself at him.

She'd just made a fool of herself. And now he was trying to get rid of her.

They walked in silence until they came to the villa.

She stepped away, too embarrassed to look him in the eye. "I must go now." She shook her head at her own stupidity and confusion.

"Come inside. I'll have someone drive you home."

"Thank you, but no. I've troubled you enough. I'll find my own way home."

"The same way you found your own way here. Tell me, why did you come?"

"I came to find someone."

"Who?"

"Conte di Montecorvio Rovella."

It was as if a shadow fell across his face. He looked toward the room, almost angry.

"You were looking for the conte. You know him?"

"Sure. I've met him a number of times. Do you know him?"

He ignored her question.

"And what do you want with the conte?"

"It's business."

"Personal business, no doubt. The conte is a lucky man. It is a shame he's proved elusive."

"Yep. Misinformed, I guess."

"I'm sorry you wasted your time on me. Presumably you had your sights set higher."

"You think I'm a gold digger?" She shook her head in sudden defeat. "You're probably right. I need his money. But it's business, not personal."

Without his funds she'd never complete the ancient Roman mosaic at her dig, never piece together the fragments of the past into one unified, beautiful, perfect whole. She chewed her lip in an effort to stem the tears that threatened. She turned away and looked up into the night sky for the same reason.

A stray gust of wind caught her shawl and it slipped, drifting down past her bare shoulders and back.

Alessandro looked at the beautiful woman, as the wrap descended in a cloud of silk, and his breath suddenly halted, his heart ached.

He had never seen such scars—luminescent white under the moonlight, pearly slivers of pain criss-crossed around her shoulders, and back. No doubt she barely felt the downward slide of the silk against the desensitized skin.

He reached his hand to touch one of the scarred shoulders, but stopped short.

"I'm sorry." He swallowed back the impulse to place a kiss where his hand had nearly touched. "Perhaps I can help. I know the conte and will arrange for you to meet with him."

She turned quickly back to face him and he dropped his hand. The beauty of her eyes, dark and passionate in the dim light took his breath away once more. What was it about this woman?

"Really? I'd appreciate it. A lot."

She looked up at him, completely unaware that the tracery of scars was on display. He focused on her beautiful eyes: eyes that could create magic, could create love, could create a future.

He turned away suddenly. He'd vowed never to live for the future or the past—always to stay in the present.

When he turned back she was standing, her wrap back in place, seemingly unaware of it having fallen. She looked at home in the luscious garden: sensual and arousing, demanding more than a physical response. But surely that was something he couldn't give?

She looked up at him, a complex blend of hope, embarrassment and pride combining in that one glance. Then she turned and began walking away.

She was different to anyone he'd ever met. Even simply in this one act. Because no woman had ever walked away from him since his wife had done so.

The thought of the resemblance cut through the heat of his passion like a blade. He'd help her if he could. But that was it. No-one, but no-one must be allowed to touch him. He had enough guilt and hurt to last him a life-time. But the sight of the scars on this beautiful woman had already cut through his defenses.

"M," he called. She stopped without turning. "Where can the conte reach you?"

"He knows."

"He may have forgotten."

"Unlikely. I'm living on his estate."

Emily didn't hear him reply. It was obvious she'd never hear from him again. And she began walking back, back to the road, back to the past. It was the only thing that mattered after all.

CHAPTER 2

*T*he midday sun glinted on the naked bodies; the chips of white marble were artfully set to give depth to the mosaic and to highlight its sensuality.

Emily's eyes followed the line of the man's thighs until they met the curve of the woman's bottom. She sat astride him, she was taking pleasure from him—her face glowed with sensual arousal, her mouth was partly open as if a moan had just escaped—but her heavy-lidded eyes were staring directly at the person observing her: the artist, Emily assumed.

It wasn't just the focus on the camera that Emily had to check. Her own perspective seemed to have altered since last night. She could see only the woman's ecstasy and the intimate connections between the couples, rather than the mosaic's artistry and antiquity. She swallowed hard, refocused the camera onto the wider scene and took the shot.

She had to have something to show the count. This undiscovered, mini-Pompeii, had lain undisturbed by the outside world for centuries, until the old count had sought her services. He'd been frail then and she'd rarely seen him.

And now months had passed without word and the money had run out.

But it seemed the man from the party, Alex, had been as good as his word and she'd received a message that she had an appointment with the elderly aristocrat.

With her camera clamped firmly to her eye, Emily ducked her head as she shuffled backwards under the overgrown canopy of grape vines and tangle of what was once a beautiful, lush garden, edging away from the subject of the camera until it was all in focus. She needed to show its extent; she needed to be persuasive.

There, she had it—the Aphrodite Mosaic—in all its incomplete glory. The mosaic was unique in terms of the scale and artistry. It was unique to Emily. She felt a deep need to see the shattered and fragile mosaic complete once more: to be as perfect as it could be, to be beautiful once more.

The artists responsible for the Aphrodite Mosaic had been trained in Athens before sailing to the Greek colonies in Italy hundreds of years before Christ—that was obvious from their technical skill—but their heart, their soul, their vision of Aphrodite could be traced directly to the local vernacular of art. It was rich, earthy and sensual.

And Emily was going to make it whole again if it was the last thing she did.

She clicked the shutter once more and let the camera fall, looking at the mosaic—only half complete, only half as beautiful as it would be.

All she needed was the money.

THE MOMENT the elevator doors swept open noiselessly Emily knew she was in trouble.

This wasn't the place for antiquity-loving people. Austere,

modern and expensive, the building screamed corporate finance. The old count didn't look the corporate type and yet it was to the Rovella Tower that she'd been told to go.

She gave her name to the receptionist and was taken directly to the top floor—the Penthouse Suite.

She smiled to herself. If the old count wanted to meet her somewhere private, as opposed to an office—a place where rational decisions were made based on economic sense— then that was OK with her.

There would be no economic return on completing the mosaic. Her mind flashed to her vision of the courtyard impressive once more: its fountains carefully repaired, its gardens restored and the mosaic—the masterpiece— painstakingly put back together using the detailed nine-teenth century drawings she'd discovered buried in the archives of the Museo Archeologico Nazionale. The pieces were all there: buried and scattered within the grounds. It would be a place of peace and beauty, a place where the past could be experienced and understood.

Her reverie was interrupted by the elevator arriving in a huge vestibule. She stepped out and hesitated, frowning. Still no personal touches, no pieces of antiquity that betrayed the count's interests. Not even in his own home?

She pushed her old-fashioned glasses back into place, smoothed the worn summer dress that was all she had in her wardrobe that was the least bit smart and walked carefully, trying to minimize the flop of her roman sandals against the marble floor. As she approached, a large oak door swung open noiselessly.

"Signorina M?" An immaculately-clad woman, with a phone clamped to her ear, didn't wait for a reply but impa-tiently clicked her fingers and beckoned Emily to enter the room.

Emily followed the woman's pointed finger and sat down

where she was told, as the woman promptly ignored her and continued to berate some poor minion with a barrage of shrill Italian. She looked around, bemused. If this was a home, it wasn't like one she'd ever seen. Sleek, minimalist and scarily officious—and that was just the woman—Emily wondered what on earth the count was doing here.

She didn't have time to form a conclusion because a man —as stressed-looking as the woman—swung open an inner door suddenly and impatiently clicked his fingers and beckoned to her.

"Now. Come!"

She jumped up and followed him into a large reception room and, again, sat down where indicated. The man promptly disappeared.

Then she heard a door open behind her and she closed her eyes in irritation.

"If anyone's about to click their fingers at me again, I'll—"

"You'll what, Miss M?"

She jumped up.

Standing before her—taller than she remembered but just as mesmerizing—was the stranger from last night.

She dropped her gaze quickly, shocked. Although he'd arranged the meeting, she hadn't expected to see him again. In fact she'd spent her day trying to forget him.

She chanced another look, only to see a flash of amusement further warm his eyes that glowed like dark amber in the rich light of a Naples evening. Their heat seemed to leap the narrow gap between them and send a flare deep inside. She took a steadying breath.

"I'm here to see the count."

She lowered her eyes and focused directly ahead—on his chest.

Unfortunately, he had on no tie and his shirt was unbuttoned. A few hairs pushed up and rested on dark, tanned skin. A vivid memory of his scent, of the feel of his skin against hers, filled her mind and her body.

"So I understand."

"I thought you'd made an appointment for me to see the count."

"I have, for Signorina M." The warmth of his eyes suddenly grew warmer, as he worked to contain a smile. "Is that really you behind those glasses?"

She could feel her skin flush. "Of course it is. I always wear them. Except—"

"Except last night when you needed to impress."

"I wish I had worn them, perhaps I wouldn't have been such an easy target."

She bit her lip. She hadn't meant to say that.

He raised an eyebrow.

"I mean—"

"I know what you mean. You appear to believe I targeted you. I tend to think it was the other way around."

Don't respond. Don't say anything. He'd be gone in a minute—presumably he was here only to introduce her to the count—and then she'd regain her sanity.

"Drink?"

She shook her head.

As he poured himself a whisky Emily looked around, trying to stifle the potentially debilitating mixture of attraction and nerves. The room had 180 degree views of the city and of the Bay of Naples, with Mount Vesuvius sitting ominously beyond. She looked away. She had her very own brand of simmering eruption.

The room was like the others except for a huge table in front of the window upon which sat scale models of a building development. She narrowed her eyes. What on earth was the count doing with these? Then she did a second-take. And why did they look vaguely familiar?

"Take a seat."

She looked directly into his eyes for the first time and struggled to retain her sense of purpose under the flicker of interest and humor she saw there. Unconsciously she pressed the palm of her hand to her stomach, where the heat lay, desperately trying to keep her body in check.

"Look, I won't waste your time and I don't want to keep the count waiting."

"You won't."

"And that would be because?"

"He's here. Waiting for you to take a seat so that he can also sit and have a drink."

"What," she said in her iciest tone, "are you talking about?"

"I am Conte di Montecorvio Rovella. I am surprised you don't recognize me as you said that you'd met him. After all, you have your glasses on today."

"*You* are the count." Her voice was quiet. The heat of attraction twisted to anger in a heartbeat. What the hell was going on? Who did he think he was fooling?

"That is correct. Now, all I need to know is why you would lie to try to see me."

She dropped into the chair and tapped her finger on its side, attempting to gain control of the confusion that ran rampant through her mind and her body. She took a deep breath.

"You're calling me a liar? And yet you had your staff contact me at the estate. You must know who I am, know that I'm not a liar." Her voice was so quiet that she could hear the soft thud of her heart.

He shrugged. "You are a worker on my estate. I haven't been there for years. You don't know me. Why did you say you did?"

"A liar," she repeated. "And yet you agreed to set up this meeting with the count. Why would you do that for a liar?"

His eyes contracted slightly but still held her gaze steadily. "Curious. Interested, maybe."

"Your life must be very dull if a meeting with a liar interests you. Or perhaps you wanted to seduce me more thoroughly this time?"

She winced as soon as the words slipped out. She didn't know what made her say it. It was stupid. But it had been the thought that she'd been trying to suppress all day: why did he pay attention to her when he could have had any woman in the room?

He smiled, a slow lazy smile that sent her heart rate up yet another notch.

"Yes, I suppose a midnight flirtation could be seen as only a partial seduction: a trial perhaps, to see if one wants to go further—or not. It seems that you would."

"I most certainly would not. But you're a man and—"

"Men always want more? Is that how you see the opposite sex? All or nothing, black or white? It seems that you have experienced little to do with seduction in your life." He leaned forward, his eyes alight with humor. "Perhaps I should show you after all. Perhaps—"

"No—"

"Please don't interrupt. You were quite correct. I should seduce you more thoroughly. Particularly as it's something you expect."

Emily shot up to her feet. "That's it. I'm going. You got me here under false pretenses. You're claiming to be the count and it's obvious you're simply playing with me. I have business to do with the count, not this nonsense."

"Now, seduction equals nonsense? Ah, *cara*, you really are in dire need of seduction." He rose too and, before she could do anything, flicked the band out from her hair, allowing it to shower down around her shoulders. He sat back down, playing with the band in his hands.

"That, is better. Now sit down and tell me what your business is with me."

She gritted her teeth and contented herself with giving him one of her glares while pushing the hair firmly behind her shoulders. "Business? You sure?"

He raised his eyebrows in mock innocence. "Of course".

She sat down warily.

"I did not lie. I met the count two years ago in London. He's passionate about Roman antiquities and a real gentleman. Which is more than can be said for you."

All humor gone, he dropped his gaze as a flicker of sadness passed over his face.

"You have described my father well. I must apologize. I assumed you were—well, let's say I jumped to conclusions." He looked up at her and, this time, she could see sadness and regret in his eyes. "I don't meet people like you very often."

"People like me? Hard working, honest? Then you've been mixing with the wrong crowd."

To her surprise, his lips parted in a relaxed smile. "Now I know that you would have got on well with my father. He was of the same mind."

Emily felt herself melt under that disarming gaze. Her breath hitched as he rose and walked towards her. Then her eyes dropped as he walked by and poured a large glass of chilled white wine.

She pushed her glasses back on her nose, even though they were still in place, and took a deep breath for control.

"Here."

"But I don't want—"

"Have it anyway. I'm afraid I need to tell you something."

She took a large gulp of wine.

"Firstly, I'm sorry to tell you what you obviously don't yet know. My father died last month."

Shock and sadness and hopelessness filled her. She slowly and deliberately placed the wine glass on the table, focusing on the movement to give herself time to absorb the fact that the erudite, very much alive, man was no more. If only she'd ventured out of the estate that was deserted except for her team, she might have discovered this fact before now. But she'd been cut off, lost in her work, oblivious to everything else. She closed her eyes as the hopelessness of her future hit her. The completion of the mosaic— the culmination of years of intensive research—had just slipped out of her grasp.

"I'm sorry for your loss," she said, somehow managing to swallow back the bitter disappointment and realize that this man had just lost his father.

"Thank you." The confident exterior flickered briefly. "Now, what can I do for you?"

She looked up into his eyes, all fight gone. "Are you interested in Roman antiquities?"

He shook his head. "They exist; they are the past and I'm not interested in the past. I'm a property developer."

"A developer?" It was scarcely credible that this man was the son of the count, someone who had treasured the past. She smiled and rose. "Well, thanks for your time. I won't waste any more of it." She nodded over to the modernist development models by the window. "It's obvious demolition and construction is more your thing."

"Wait." He touched her arm with his hand, too gently to stop her. He didn't need force anyway, not with the effect his body had on hers. She turned and faced him, searching his face, trying to find some explanation for the bone-deep attraction she felt for him.

He didn't speak immediately. The low evening sun flickered across his jaw, his muscle clenching as though indi-cating an inner tension.

"I want to help. Tell me, first, how you knew my father."

She let out a breath she didn't even know she was hold-ing. The tension had been reconciled somehow. The mood had changed.

"I'm an archaeologist working on the Aphrodite Mosaic and Roman courtyard at the Rovella estate. I've made progress but run out of the funds that my university and the generosity of the count gave me. I need funding to complete the dig."

"*You're* the archaeologist?"

"Yes. I've been working on the estate for the past year."

"Emily Carlyle. Of course. I didn't know."

"You haven't been there. The place has been shut up except for the estate cottages that the count allowed us to use."

"And you like it there?"

"The work is incredible—there's nothing like it—the mosaics are a real find."

"But do you like it there—the estate?"

"Of course, who wouldn't? It's beautiful, so peaceful, so quiet, a place where you can think, where the past really comes alive."

"Quite." His voice was suddenly chilly, distant. He rose slowly and walked across the room, looking down at the model of buildings. "I haven't been there for many years. But..." He turned to look at her suddenly; a brief, heart-melting smile flashed across his face. "But, as it happens my father has left part of his legacy for the purposes of restoring the villa estate. It's yours."

She looked up shocked, at a loss for words for once.

"If you still want it."

"Of course I want it. It's my life."

"One part of your life, maybe. It's yours but there are certain conditions."

She narrowed her eyes suspiciously. "And they are?"

"It is part of my father's bequest that the archaeologist in charge of the dig stays on site."

"I'll stay with the others at the cottages on the edge of the estate. They're fine for our needs."

"No, if you want the money, you'll stay at the villa. I'll make sure it's comfortable for you."

"Where I stay is none of your concern. I'll be hired for my professional services alone."

"That's fine, Emily—may I call you Emily?" He smiled at her glower. "Well, Emily," he eased himself back in the chair, "if you don't wish to stay in the villa, we will simply find another archaeologist to take over the dig. I'm sure there are any number of unemployed archaeologists eager to get their teeth into something like this. Shame, that you'd let one small thing stand between you and the opportunity to cement your reputation."

"You're blackmailing me."

"Me? I'm not doing anything. No, my father created the conditions of his will. It's he who wanted the archaeologist to stay in the villa. Perhaps for sentimental purposes, perhaps for practical—who knows? But if anyone's doing anything, it's him. But then, he's not around to do anything about it. We're stuck with it. Do you honestly think I want some stranger in my family home?"

"You're never there. The place hasn't been lived in since your father left."

"Beside the point. You want this or not?"

"Of course I want it."

"Then I will make sure my staff make you comfortable."

"And the money?"

"It'll be paid monthly to ensure your compliance with the terms of the will. I will need to be sure—will need proof."

"You're going to have someone check my room to make sure I'm sleeping in it?"

"Now, there you have given me an idea. But who should I trust?"

"This is ridiculous."

"This is your one and only opportunity to complete the dig. Take it or leave it."

"I take it of course."

Emily had to fight to control her anger.

"For a woman who has just succeeded in her mission, you appear to be unhappy."

Emily could feel her whole body trembling with anger and frustration. And she could see that he didn't understand her reaction.

But how could he? He would never have experienced what she'd gone through—the sort of humiliating and destructive control that had sworn her off men for life. How was he to know that she'd worked hard—years of study and research, years where her only down time was spent with her cat—to make sure that she could never be hurt again?

And yet here she was, vulnerable once more.

"I am happy to get the job and to be able to complete the most beautiful assignment that I shall ever come across. But you've used your power to force me to live away from my team, on my own, far from the nearest neighbor. *That* does not make me happy. *That* does not make me comfortable."

"You will be safe enough. It is a secure estate. There is nothing to fear."

"Sure." She flicked him a brief, tight smile. "So, that's it? Nothing else you need to know?"

"You surely don't expect me to give away thousands of dollars without seeing where it's going?"

"You said it wasn't your thing."

"Money is my thing. I will see you at the estate tomorrow. I'll expect you to show me what progress has been made."

"You want to see progress? I can show you progress. I have photos." She shook them out of her bag and spread them in front of him on the table.

He picked up one of the photos, his expression absorbed. "You've worked hard. I haven't seen these for over twenty years when they were half buried by overgrown vines, and so incomplete as to make no sense."

He looked up at her for the first time with a respect and interest that disarmed Emily completely, making her instantly forget the restrictive conditions of the grant.

"How did you know about them in the first place? Even my father was unaware of them until several years ago."

He indicated the chair and she sat without thinking, her passion for her subject overtaking all thought and feeling.

"Research—thorough research, both in London and Rome and the archives in Naples. From the old documents I knew it existed and roughly where it was. And then I found it. Ah!" she exhaled quickly, "you should see it, its exquisite. Nothing like it exists. Even the best at Pompeii has nothing on it. It will cause a sensation."

"And make your career, I should imagine."

She shook her head, his cynicism bringing her back to earth. How could she expect him—a corporate developer—to understand?

"I'm not doing it for my career. I have work lined up for the next decade if I want it. I have a tenured university position. That isn't why I'm doing this."

"Why then?"

Their eyes connected and she moved her mouth as if to begin to explain. But how could she? She'd hardly expressed it clearly to herself. There was something about the need to complete this work of art—to make it whole again—that was so instinctive that she couldn't put it in words.

She shrugged. "I just do. I have a *feeling* for it."

"Yes, I can see that."

His eyes descended to her arms and she self-consciously plucked at her short-sleeved dress to cover the lower edges of her scars. Normally she never worried about them. But for some reason she didn't want him to see. Not this man, this perfect man. He wouldn't appreciate anything broken. And for some unknown reason she wanted to be appreciated by him.

She pulled off her glasses slowly, bit her lip as she rubbed them desultorily on her dress, before she popped them, loose, in her bag. She wanted to see his reaction. And, when she did, she was gratified—and annoyed at the same time.

The slow smile, the darkening appreciation of his eyes as they looked into hers. She was correct. The perfect man was only attracted to the perfect woman. Shame he'd gone all blurry with the removal of her glasses. Ironic really. The only way she could be appreciated was if she couldn't appreciate him. Which did she want most?

The glasses remained in the bag as she rose and made for the door.

"I'll show you the rest of the site tomorrow."

His eyes all but devoured her, a predator once more.

"I'll look forward to it."

How did he manage to convey so much meaning in a few innocuous words?

She walked quickly into the outer office, aware that they were now completely alone.

As he stretched over her shoulder and pressed the button to the elevator, his body brushed hers. The smell of his skin, so indefinably warm and male, sent a signal straight to her gut and she inhaled sharply.

She stared, unseeing, out the window as the sun dipped below the horizon that fringed the Bay of Naples.

He followed her gaze.

"Vesuvius. So perfect and yet so deadly."

"Never trust perfection." She hoped he couldn't hear the tremor in her voice.

"Si, decisamente."

She stepped into the elevator and watched him turn away from her before the doors closed.

ALESSANDRO STOOD by the window ten floors up and watched Emily walk swiftly from the building. No taxi for her, he smiled to himself, as she walked towards the station: independent, intelligent and extremely interesting.

He sat down, put his feet on the table and downed a mouthful of whisky.

He'd wondered what his father had been up to with this particular bequest but he'd been reluctant to investigate by returning to the estate that held so many memories. The old rogue. So that was his game.

Lure him back to the old world, entice him with a beautiful woman—for his father had been quite clear in his will that the post should be given to only one person, Miss Carlyle—and do what his father hadn't been able to do over the past five years. Make him stand still and remember.

He swirled the amber liquid around in the glass. He drank too much, he knew. But he didn't want to remember. And with Emily as a diversion, surely he wouldn't have to?

Because there was one small thing that he hadn't told Emily about his father's bequest. He would be spending more time with her than she thought.

CHAPTER 3

*E*mily straightened her back slowly, groaned and pressed a grubby hand to her temple. Trouble was, it wasn't just her back that ached. Her head throbbed through the tortuous arguments that had been raging all day.

She'd never met a man like Alessandro before.

She'd never wanted a man like Alessandro before.

And there was no way that she could ever have Alessandro.

Men like that didn't want women like her: women without charm or beauty. Once, she'd believed they did and she'd been proved spectacularly wrong. Anyway, she hadn't spent ten years immersed in her studies, in the past, in shoring up the defenses around her heart to let them break down now.

She closed her eyes against the crimson sunset that showered light through the overgrown garden and soaked up the peace. The quiet of the evening was disturbed only by the sounds of insects, birds and the water that still flowed through the Roman watercourse to the fountain: not cracked and broken, like so many things.

Alone once more. And that was the way she liked it, she reminded herself.

That way was best.

But the stirrings in her body defied her need to feel nothing. Damn.

She rubbed her eyes, tired from a day of straining over tesserae unearthed in the dig. It was difficult to stop; there was always the tantalizing hope of adding one more piece to the puzzle that was the Aphrodite Mosaic. Held up against the waning light, the small shard of amber sparkled like fire, like the fire depicted in the mosaic. Another piece. She sat back on her heels, absorbed in the beauty of the sliver of stone, hauled by oxen from the Baltic Sea over two and a half centuries before.

"All alone? I thought I was paying for a team of workers."

She jumped as if an electrical charge had shot through her body. She knew he'd come but had assumed, as the day faded, that he'd visit the next day—in daylight. She closed her eyes briefly, took a deep breath and dropped the trowel, using the seconds it took to shake herself free of the shock that still thrilled through her body.

"It's evening. Of course I'm alone. My team's gone back for supper."

"And the boss doesn't get to eat?"

She turned her head briefly. "The boss always gets to eat —but later. It's still light and, well—"

"You couldn't resist."

She grimaced to herself, closing her eyes briefly at the accuracy of his observation and turned around properly, still focusing on the stone that glowed in her hands, rather than on Alessandro. It was bad enough hearing his voice, feeling his closeness, without meeting his eyes.

"True enough. I guess it's like doing a giant jigsaw puzzle —one that no-one has done before—it's hard to stop."

"Not for everyone. Jigsaw puzzles never held any compulsion for me—other than to mix them with water and create something new." He scuffed some of the discarded rocks aside with his foot. "Such things do not interest me."

"Figures." She couldn't draw her eyes away from him, standing there amidst the overgrown vines and trees. He should have looked incongruous—with his expensive clothes, his city ways—but he didn't. The predator looked at home. "But you found me OK. It's not exactly easy to find your way around the estate—everything is so overgrown."

He looked up from the ground and his complex look of ruefulness, as if caught out, flipped her stomach.

"Easy for me. I was raised here, by my grandparents. This," he gestured around the wilderness that was, centuries ago, a formal garden, "was my playground".

"Must have been magic."

"For a child maybe. But children find magic anywhere." He looked her intently in the eyes, surely a look practiced for seduction. "I'm sure you did."

A vision of the concrete forecourt of the council estate in which she grew up flashed into her mind.

"Why do you think that?"

Somehow he'd come closer to her. He stood before the setting sun, as it dipped below the bleached hills. The radiance around his head created a shadow and mystery to his face. She could feel the warmth of the crimson light on her face and she blinked, whether at his proximity or the light, she couldn't have said.

"You have a strength about you, a light." His eyes narrowed, assessingly. "I think your surroundings impact on you only as much as you want them to. Your reality is what you want it to be."

A further vision of raking away the overgrown grasses that tufted between the cracked pavers of the concrete playground entered her head. She used to collect treasures she found there—money, beads, once even a family photo—things that made up a life. She used to imagine that they were from her real home—the one where her parents were still alive—not the place she lived with her foster family. And she'd been looking for that home her whole life.

"Maybe." She suddenly felt uncomfortable. "The trouble with magic, is that it never lasts."

"It wouldn't be magic if it did." He picked up the trowel that she'd just dropped. "And this is the instrument of your magic these days?"

"Yes." He was getting too close. She had to shift the focus back to him. "I wonder what yours is?"

"Probably this." He tossed his phone lightly into the air. "Couldn't live without it."

"That's not magic, that's work."

"It creates my world and *that* is not all work, believe me."

She did. The sparkle in his eyes spoke volumes. She felt his hedonistic pleasure in life reach out to her and try to draw her in. She could almost believe for one moment that he was here for pleasure, to see her. His eyes certainly gave that message—warm and interested. And his talk—of her, of her life—what was that if not flirtation? And it was working. Through every tiny fiber, every muscle, every nerve of her body, it was working.

She couldn't help responding to his slow smile with one of her own.

He stepped towards her and handed her back the trowel. "But it's business I'm here for today, of course."

She stepped away as if trying to stop a physical connection.

"Of course." He wasn't here for pleasure. This was business. That was where she came in. "I'll show you around."

"After you."

Alessandro pulled back a branch of an overgrown orange tree, its blossom ghostly and its scent overpowering in the twilight.

She turned on the torch and walked past him, her bare arm accidentally touching his.

Her eyes flicked up to his in acknowledgement of the mutual charge that had been ignited before she quickly turned away. He followed her down the tunnel-like path, tamped down by the team of archaeologists, but surrounded by the overgrown trees and undergrowth of centuries of neglect.

She stopped abruptly at the edge of the clearing and he looked around with interest. He remembered it as a child. Despite the overgrown vegetation he'd managed to make a tunnel through to a small part of the ruin. Not that he had been interested in ancient ruins, only in getting out of trouble, of hiding where no-one could find him.

"You know much about all this?"

Her voice was hushed, intimate, in the secluded setting. They were in an enclosed area, surrounded by overgrown shrubbery, and beyond, the dark hills encircled them in absolute secrecy. The tone of her voice seemed to vibrate directly to him across the paved surfaces of the Roman remains, sending a flicker of sensation across his skin.

What was it about this woman that touched him so? She was no seductress. With her large old-fashioned glasses covering her face, her hair drawn back severely, and her boyish shirt, shorts and sandals, she would have been invisible among the crowds of tourists who flocked to Pompeii. He watched her turn in the direction of the mosaic. The strong line of her determined chin, a challenge; the full lips that lay lightly parted, an invitation. She turned, obviously wondering why he did not reply. He cleared his throat and stepped over to her.

"No. It was just a place where one could hide from trouble. The cold marble under your body on a hot day, the trees overhead: a good hiding place. I don't even think my grandparents were aware of it."

She shone the torch on to a small part of the unfinished mosaic depicting a goddess clothed in flowers and gold.

"This is where the lady of the house would have slept. Each of the rooms has a different character. This is the real find. The Aphrodite Mosaic." She approached it and touched it with her fingertips, trailing them over the lumpy surface like a lover. "Isn't it wonderful? They've used all kinds of tesserae to get the subtle colors and shades. It's so delicate, so—."

"Incomplete."

She pursed her lips. "But it won't be. It might have been forgotten about in your parents' and grandparents' time but thanks to your nineteenth-century ancestors we've discovered very fine, detailed drawings that show exactly how it should look. Otherwise, I couldn't do the work. I'm finding whole sections that simply need to be carefully replaced. There are only small parts that need to be filled up from the tiny pieces scattered around here." She stopped suddenly as if conscious that her passion for her work was making her talk too much. "It will be beautiful," she added softly.

"It is beautiful," he corrected. "It reminds me of the Persephone Mosaic in Napoli for its delicacy."

"We think it's the same artist; must have been Greek, around 200 BC."

He whistled. "It'll be valuable then."

She looked up at him sharply. "Of course. It will contribute so much to our knowledge of the period. And we can keep it in situ, show people how it was used in context." She shone her light into an adjoining room. "And here, people at leisure, theatre, sports. It all helps piece together the past of the people who once lived here."

"And there are other rooms, are there not? I seem to remember as a boy, discovering a part of a wall mosaic that proved particularly interesting to a young boy." He took her hand and tilted the flash light across to the other side of the dig, beyond which a spring still bubbled, feeding the water-course and fountain. "Show me."

"There's plenty more to see here." She crouched on the floor. "Look at the—"

"Show me the bathhouse."

She flashed a look of irritation over her glasses. He could read her thoughts as if she'd said them aloud.

Emily clamped her mouth shut. Trust a man to be more interested in the "sex" mosaic as her team called it, rather than in the subtle beauty of the Aphrodite Mosaic.

"Sure."

She walked carefully across the dig, making sure she didn't disturb the current excavations until they came to one large room. It stood central to the house—the remains of a loggia revealed that it opened out onto the courtyard where the fountains and gardens would have provided an appropriate aesthetic backdrop to the sensual leisure activities of the masters and mistresses.

She shone the torch on one of the central pieces that had survived intact. It was even more graphic than the couple making love that she'd been working on earlier. That at least had been sensual, its artistry subtle and its colors muted. It had been created for a woman's pleasure in the lady's bedroom.

There was nothing subtle about the bathhouse mosaic. Emily willed herself to keep the torch shining on the tumble of naked women who were all over an overly endowed man. With wild expressions, they pressed their naked bodies to his, while others had turned to each other for satisfaction and yet others laid siege to him with their mouths. This time it was the man who looked directly to the viewer. But his face showed a satisfaction that had little to do with sensuality; it was all about power.

"That's what you wanted to see."

"Yes." He approached it, interested. "You've done a lot of work to it. It's much clearer now." He stood back, as if to appreciate it better.

"Yes, well…" She tried not to sound as embarrassed as she felt. "I guess it would intrigue the adolescent imagination." She jerked her hand away from his, turning the light on the ground on which they stood. The mosaic floor shone under its beam revealing safe, geometric patterns.

Alessandro was irritated by her attitude.

"Not just the adolescent—it was meant to entertain the people who came here for their leisure." He couldn't resist stepping closer to her, pushing the boundaries of her silence. "For sex."

She stepped away and leaned against a pillar that had once led to the room. "Yes, of course. And it's beautifully executed."

"You seem a little nervous." He watched as her hands absent-mindedly ran along the carvings on the surface of the pillar. It seems that she'd temporarily forgotten that it, too, depicted symbols that indicated the room's use.

"No, just appreciating the finer points of the mosaic."

"I appreciate all the points of the mosaic." He looked around. The moon had just risen, making the flashlight redundant. He leaned over to her—sensing her stayed breath, her response to him—took her hand and turned off the flashlight. "I don't think we need this now."

He bent his head close to hers, enjoying the sweetness of her breath against his mouth.

She swallowed. "So, have you seen enough?"

He shook his head. "Not nearly enough."

He should, but he couldn't resist. That was what his life was all about, wasn't it? Pleasure. The moment. It had served him well for five years. And would for another five, regardless of what his departed father appeared to have had in mind.

His eyes scanned her face, taking in the blend of nerves and attraction in her eyes, despite the moon's silver sheen that bounced off her glasses.

He moved his finger around her wide cheekbones and under her glasses.

"Why do you wear these?"

"Short sighted."

"But there is nothing far away for you to see here. There is just me."

"And you need to keep far away."

"Then why are you not moving back?"

She shook her head half-heartedly as if confused.

He smiled as he felt, rather than saw, her shift her face imperceptibly towards his.

To think that he'd anticipated being holed up in this God-forsaken place with some dry, ancient academic. She was his to take. He could see that any lingering resistance on her part had evaporated. He could only imagine her body, readying itself for him. He cupped the back of her head and gently brought her lips to his own. Barely a flutter, barely a touch, before pulling away.

Hardly a kiss. Something he'd done thousands of times before without a thought.

Perhaps it was the thin light of the moon that drained the place of its reality; perhaps it was the scent of her—no perfume, only herself—or perhaps he'd just grown tired.

Whatever, something was different.

He felt it viscerally. It was like the brief twist of a kaleido-scope, imperceptibly moving, but changing everything forever. The world had shifted and a different pattern had emerged from its chaos.

But some things were still the same.

He still wanted her: charmed by her honesty, seduced by her body, interested by her mind.

Except now, this woman had become something more—something to be treasured.

He stepped back abruptly. He had no room in his life—in his heart—for treasures. You took what you were given, you developed, and you moved on. Taking the profits of the moment and moving onto the next one.

No keepers. Ever.

He took another step back.

"Emily, we should go now. I've seen enough."

She nodded and looked down. Even with those hideous glasses he could see the hurt and confusion that filled her eyes before she dipped her head.

He'd done it. He'd seduced her—with a little help from the ethereal ruins that surrounded them and the light that bathed them both in a surreal glamour—he had her in the palm of his hands.

But he didn't want her now. She was too dangerous.

She turned away from him—in defense he knew—and he watched as she bent down, turned on the torch and brushed off some dirt that had fallen onto the tesserae. With her body in darkness and her strong profile clearly outlined by the light, Alessandro felt her presence as if it were his own.

Aghast, he turned away and waited while she scooped up a couple of stray trowels, took one last look around and started walking carefully towards the pathway.

He followed silently.

Emily ignored the brush of creepers across her face,

pushing any that obstructed her path gently out of the way with cool deliberation. There was to be no damage done to the gardens—her dig had definite parameters, outside of which nothing must be touched. These were the conditions of the dig.

Everything had its secrets that should not be disturbed until it was time to reveal them. And so did everyone.

So what were his secrets that made him change so abruptly? Or perhaps he had none?

He'd regretted the kiss—that much was obvious. Then what made him do it? She hadn't asked for one, had she? She wasn't all dressed up in someone else's clothes, trying to look glamorous, trying to look seductive, was she?

She could feel the cold anger building by increments, with each damning thought.

Perhaps he'd just lost interest. Perhaps it had all been about the thrill of the chase. Well, the chase hadn't lasted long in her case—her defenses had been shot since the first time she'd seen him.

But she was angry, because while he might regret it, she couldn't.

The night was hot and humid. It throbbed with the hum and trill of insects, the whir of bat wings and the rustle of night creatures. The sultry air seemed to clog in her throat. She wanted to get out and fast.

She pressed on, shining the torch ahead of them, keeping to the fragile path through the tangle of vegetation that kept the dig hidden, keeping one step ahead of him, trying to widen the gap but failing.

She had to get away. But she could hear him moving behind her, she could sense his eyes upon her and all she could do was pray that he would disappear as soon as she reached the villa and leave her to her own thoughts and regrets.

They emerged abruptly into the pool of a gas light that the staff had lit for her. She turned at the entrance and faced him squarely.

"Goodnight. I won't keep you from rushing back to civilization. You know that I'm keeping to the terms of your father's will. I think that's pretty much concludes our business."

"No, there's something else. Go inside, I will talk to you there."

"No you won't. I want a bath and then I want to eat. And I want you to go—now."

"We need to talk."

"You might. But I don't."

She didn't wait to listen or see his response but entered the courtyard and walked quickly into the huge kitchen where her dinner was laid out.

Her eyes narrowed. The table was set for two.

She looked around to find Alessandro standing at the door.

"As I said. We have things to discuss."

"You're playing games with me. I didn't ask for it and I don't like it."

He pulled out a chair for her to sit.

"Unfortunately for us both, it is not me playing the games."

"What the hell are you talking about? Don't mess with me, Conte di Montecorvio Rovella. You may have the grand title but I can look after myself."

He pulled out a chair and sat down, pouring himself a glass of the chilled white wine. "I don't doubt it. But it won't be necessary. And, please, call me Alessandro.'

"I'll call you what the hell I like. Now, get out." She could barely stop herself from shaking.

"May I remind you that this is my home." His tone was

calm, disinterested almost. It inflamed Emily's temper even further.

"Yes, but why would you stay here when you have no interest in antiquities, no interest in me—which you've made patently clear—or this estate."

"You are wrong there."

Emily swallowed. Could he really be still interested in her?

"How so?"

"I have a deep interest in this estate, for one thing."

"And for another?" Her soft words almost drowned in the heavy, ancient atmosphere of the huge room.

"And for another, I have no choice but to be here."

"Believe me. You do. If it's my security you're worried about, don't be. I'm a big girl and can look after myself." She walked to the door. "Go. Go now."

He didn't even bother to reply. She heard the chair scrape against the terracotta tiles of the kitchen floor and then she started under his touch.

Frustration was driving her crazy and she could feel tears pressing against her closed lids.

"Please."

"Emily, I cannot. I, like you, will also be staying in the villa."

Emily slapped his hand away, fierce anger taking over from despair.

"You most certainly will not. You've made me stay here against my will. And now, you say, what? That you're also going to be staying here? There is no-one else here after 5pm. We will be alone."

"And why does that scare you? You think you are so desirable that I cannot control myself. I apologize for the kiss in the garden and assure you there will be no repetition."

"I wonder if you realize what an insulting bastard you are."

She watched as he pushed his hands through his hair as if in confusion.

"I do not mean to be, Emily." His voice was softer now. "I cannot explain. I can only apologize. It is nothing to do with you. But me. It is me who cannot do this. But I am stuck here. As you say, I would prefer to be in Naples—or preferably New York or London—but I am here for the next three months."

"What?"

"It is my father's will. For me to inherit the estate I must also stay here."

He stood close: so close that she could see the flicker of tension in his cheek, could see the agitation in his eyes, and could, above all, feel her attraction drawing her to him. Did she move? She couldn't have said, but she felt his hand reach out as if to stop her. Or him.

"We have no choice."

He dropped his hand, shook his head and walked away. The door, caught by a draught of cool night air, slammed shut behind him.

Emily felt its vibration throughout her body. But she hardly knew whether it came from within or without.

It echoed around the empty villa.

And it closed something deep inside.

CHAPTER 4

"Come on Em. Something's up, so tell me."

Emily scowled at her assistant, Sue, and looked back down at the laptop.

"How do you feel?" Sue persisted.

Numb.

That was the only word Emily could use to describe how she felt—or rather how she felt nothing whatsoever. Even working on the mosaic failed to give her the buzz of excitement that it always had. And her team had obviously noticed.

"I'm working," she growled, and stabbed her finger on to the delete key to remove the offending email.

"So what's this count like?"

Her heart thudded painfully, reminding Emily of the reason that she'd battened down her feelings.

"Fantastic."

"Really?"

"Yeah, he got the generator and the internet connection set up, didn't he?"

"So what's up with you, then?"

"Don't you ever stop?"

Sue grinned. "Nope. That's what you taught me. When you're on the scent of something, keep going."

"Yeah, well, you're not the only one on the scent of something."

"What do you mean?"

"The word's out about this dig. We'll have every man and his dog sniffing around now." Emily leaned back against the tree, sighed and rubbed her hands over her face. She was tired. She hadn't slept well all week.

She snapped the laptop shut and stood up.

"Look, get the team moving, we've less time than we thought now. I need to see to something."

Sue's mouth opened as if to reply but she obviously thought better of it and returned to work.

THE SUN WAS high as Emily drove down the narrow, winding road to the bottom of the valley. Steep sides swept down treed ravines to the valley far below. Emily opened the windows, and the air was soon filled with the dry, clogging smell of the hot, white dust that settled in a fine film on in the inside of the car. She preferred the heat, the smells, the dust of the road even, to the dry, pristine chill of air conditioning. The gravel road was difficult to negotiate, with its rutted surface and frequent rock falls on the near side of the hill. But its very inaccessibility had preserved the estate's privacy, and its treasures, for thousands of years.

Until now.

Damn. So they all knew. She'd done her best to keep the dig a secret.

She could do without the publicity.

Next she'd have the press, the universities, the authorities, even people wanting to steal the treasures, down on her and she wouldn't have a moment's peace to do her work—the only thing that was important.

She could do without the distractions.

When she reached the car park on the outskirts of the city she pulled over, turned off the engine and gently rested her head on the steering wheel, suddenly exhausted.

But it wasn't any of those reasons that gave her the flutter of fear in her gut and the tension headache that threatened to mount. It wasn't any of those reasons that had made her leave England in the first place and take the extended sabbatical.

She sat back and pushed her fingertips under her shirt around her shoulders, massaging the raised and puckered skin that was a result of her ex-boyfriend's attack ten years ago.

A vision of his smoothly handsome face, a baby face topped with ice-blue eyes, filled her mind.

A shudder of fear and revulsion swept through her body.

He would be free of the hospital where he'd spent his jail term by now and she knew, just knew, that he'd come for her. For years he'd written to her but she'd never opened his letters, had put them straight in the bin. A few years ago his letters had stopped arriving. She didn't query it; she was just thankful. Although she'd had no contact with him, or the authorities, about his release she knew the date and he'd have been free now for a month. He'd come for her all right.

And now he knew where she was.

Who had told? Who else knew?

Her professor? He had no reason to tell.

Her staff? Also no reason. It was in all of their best interests to keep the dig quiet.

That left Conte di Montecorvio Rovella. The elusive count. And wasn't she glad he was elusive? She hadn't seen him for the past week. Gone before she'd risen—and she rose early—and arriving back after she'd gone to bed. Only the smell of fresh coffee and aftershave lingered in the morning.

Yes, she was relieved he wasn't there. It was only the pungent smell of coffee that made her breathe deeply in the mornings, several large intakes of breath. Only coffee.

She sighed.

So why would Aless— the count, the only other person who knew, tell the media?

Her gaze rose above the traffic, shooting into Naples on the motorway, to where the high-rise buildings—among which was the Rovella Tower—soared into the hot sky, dwarfed by the mass of Vesuvius that slumbered behind them.

She didn't know why, but she was damn well going to find out.

Within minutes she'd joined the throng of people on the side-walk: people shouting, motor-scooters rushing by, life everywhere.

She smiled to herself, despite the dull ache of her suppressed emotions, because she loved this city full of life and energy: its confusion of sounds, sights and smells. Not least its mouth-watering smells, Emily considered, stopping suddenly. The siren fragrance of freshly-baked pizzas and pastries made her mouth water.

Yep, she'd find out why the count had told the world about the dig—she inhaled the exquisite aroma once more—right after she'd bought lunch.

"Do you have an appointment?" The receptionist raised a thinly-plucked eyebrow, but managed to retain her mouth in a tight straight line.

"No."

"Then you can't see him." The girl pressed a button and resumed her phone call.

Emily wondered if it was company policy to reserve smiles for the rich and influential.

"You can't help me?"

"Assolutamente no."

"Then, I'll call him." She fished the phone out of her hessian bag, waved it briefly in front of the other woman's face, and plucked the business card she'd found at the estate and dialed his number.

"Where did you get that card?" demanded the receptionist.

"Oh, this? Picked it up from home. It must have fallen out of his pocket when he left in a hurry this morning."

Without waiting to enjoy the receptionist's face—she wasn't one for gloating, well not much—she turned to the floor to ceiling windows that overlooked the city and beyond to a sliver of blue sea.

"Si?" The voice was gruff. "Who is this?"

"It's the woman you're living with."

She glanced over her shoulder at the receptionist to check out the effect of her words. She turned back to the view with a smile on her face.

"What's the problem? Can't it wait until tonight?"

"No. I need to see you now. Something's come up."

"I'm busy."

"I'll wait."

She heard him exhale angrily down the phone and turn and speak in rapid Italian to someone. "Come up."

The receptionist's phone buzzed and, with a glare, she opened the private elevator for Emily.

. . .

THIS TIME there was no barrage of staff to confront her, only an angry looking Alessandro, his eyes dark under a frown and his mouth, a firm line.

"This had better be good."

"If it were good, then I wouldn't need to speak to you."

He held the door open for her and she was once more struck by how incongruous he looked—no tie, shirt open, sleeves rolled up—in the sterile atmosphere of the building and apartment.

Silently he offered her a chair and sat down opposite. She looked at him quickly and then looked down at the paper bag in her hands, unable to meet his gaze. She cleared her throat and willed herself to look up at him. This time, his eyes had warmed and his lips quirked in a smile, obviously finding her discomfort amusing. He sat back in the seat with a resigned sigh.

"Would you like a coffee, Emily? I see you brought pastries."

She glanced down at the tell-tale paper bag. "My lunch."

"Not your lunch now. You interrupt my meeting; you can share your food."

"Shame millionaires can't afford to organize their own snacks."

"I'm not a millionaire."

"Oh!" Genuinely surprised, she met his eyes for the first time. "I just thought with all this," she swept her hand around, "and the estate," she shrugged.

He narrowed his eyes in mock annoyance. "Emily. I'm far wealthier than a millionaire but probably less wealthy than people imagine—people other than yourself, obviously."

"Obviously. Here," she pushed the bag onto the table between them "I wouldn't want to make a billionaire go hungry."

He selected a lemony sfogliatelle and sat back.

"So how's the dig going?"

"Very well. You should drop by some time."

"There's no need. It's obviously in capable hands. So, if the dig's OK, what's the problem?"

"*You* are actually. Why have you told the media all about it? Do you know what this means?"

"Of course. It means interest. And interest, publicity, is always good for business."

"Yours, perhaps, not mine. What about the academics, amateurs, the media who will come flocking in, interfering with my work."

"It's private land. They can't."

"You don't know these people. They may be professional people—most of them—but they're driven. They'll be scaling that wall like it's nothing. It's not hard to climb."

She turned and looked suddenly at Alessandro, guilt causing her face to redden.

He looked at her from above his coffee cup and sat back, consideringly. "So that's how you first discovered the mosaic."

"Might have done." She crossed her arms defensively and turned back to view the bay—a brilliant blue foil to the soft yellow buildings of Naples. "Whatever. Your father was quite cool about it."

"Come on, Emily. You can cope with interest. I'd like to see anyone try to get involved. You'd send them away, no problem. So, what's this all about?"

"What about the fortune hunters, the unscrupulous, the people out to steal things, smuggle them out of Italy? They're not going to bowl along in daylight and be polite."

"I've got it covered. I've ordered security patrols, day and night."

She rolled her eyes. "Oh, that's great. I'm now living in a prison."

"Come on. That's what you say you want."

"What I want, Alessandro," she leaned across the table towards him, her eyes blazing, "is to be allowed to complete the dig in peace. What I want is to—"

"You want the dig to yourself." He also leaned forward until their faces were almost touching. "You want it for personal reasons. Because your response, Miss M," he pushed a thick strand of sun-bleached hair that had escaped her ponytail, back behind her ear, "is not the response of a professional. There's more to it than that, isn't there?"

She sunk back onto the black leather couch. "Quit the psychoanalysis. It's my work. That's all."

"So, why have you come here? The news is public. There's nothing I can do about that except to double security, which I've done. What else do you want?"

Her mouth was dry as he made her realize the real reason why she was there.

"Alessandro, you've left me vulnerable. When I'm not at the dig, I'm alone in the villa from dawn to well after dusk."

"Surely it's the treasures they're after. They won't come inside. Besides, there are the guards who will also be keeping an eye on the villa."

"Yep." She dropped her eyes and scooped up her bag from where she'd dropped it on the floor. "You're right. Don't know why I'm making the fuss."

"Emily. You are not the kind of woman to make a fuss. What is this really about?"

She bit her lip. No way in this world could she tell him— Mr Perfect—about her problems. But there was something about his tone; the authoritative note was gone, the voice was lower. He sounded almost sympathetic.

"Nothing I can't handle. Sorry to have wasted your time."

"Wait." He stood up, his hand on her arm. "Besides, Emily, *I* am there. You are not alone."

She turned to face him. That was a joke. The man had turned tail after kissing her—a mistake obviously. She wasn't in his league and she could have told him that right from the beginning.

Except she'd hoped, that just for once, she might be wrong.

"Alessandro. You're never there."

She turned and left without a backward glance.

EMILY LOVED this time of day.

The team had left. She enjoyed their company but was always glad when they'd gone and she was left alone to savor the progress of the dig, to enjoy the magic of the estate. Except now, for the first time since she'd arrived, she felt an underlying flutter of apprehension. What if her ex-boyfriend turned up?

The last time she'd seen him was ten years ago when her evidence had sealed his fate: imprisonment in a mental health facility for ten years. But now his time was up and he was free to do whatever he wanted.

He had always been a control freak—a very convincing, charming, educated, control freak. He'd set her on the academic path, given her her first break and come to control every aspect of her life until even that hadn't been enough. She hadn't seen the attack coming.

Short and violent, but with long-lasting consequences, it had taken her years of therapy to even begin to recover.

She was stronger now. But what if he turned up and she crumpled once more? She couldn't go back to those days of darkness.

She shook her head as if to rid it of the taunting thoughts. She was stronger than that, she told herself sternly.

The rich colors of the short, triumphant twilight of

southern Italy fell around her as she made her way back through the estate gardens to the villa. She stopped suddenly on the edge of the shrubbery, listening.

The simple elegance of Bach's cello suite rose and fell across the sunken gardens, its poignant tones caught on the soft evening breeze.

Someone was in the house. No-one should be there.

She clenched her fists and unclenched them, hesitating for one second before pressing on across the gardens to the villa.

She could hear the blood pounding in her ears, almost drowning out the music. The soft light of candles flickered through the open windows and she could smell the wonderful aroma of dinner. The dinner the staff left for her was usually cold. She hesitated. Since when had her ex ever cooked?

She pushed open the French windows even wider and stepped inside. Seated across the other side of the room was Alessandro, nursing a large whisky and a frown.

Relief swamped her. Despite whatever had gone on between them she felt an instinctive trust in this man.

"Alessandro! To what do I owe the pleasure?"

He raised his eyebrow at her remark. "I decided to return home early today."

She walked to the table and lifted the silver cloches from the serving dishes, sniffing appreciatively.

"Good of you considering you don't seem to like spending time here. Or perhaps it's me you've been avoiding?"

"Emily, now, why would I do that?"

"You tell me? I guess you don't much like my company."

He laughed. "You don't play around, do you Emily?"

"Play?"

"With words. You always say what you mean."

"Of course. What's the point in doing anything else?" She sat down at the table and began serving out the dinner. He rose and joined her, seating himself opposite.

He smiled again. "None. But that doesn't seem to stop the rest of your sex playing games." He uncorked the chilled bottle of white wine and poured two glasses.

"So, from the woman who doesn't play games, why are you here?"

"So, from the man who enjoys a game or two, I am here because it is my home, I am required to be here and because of something you said earlier."

"Really? You mean I said something that you actually listened to?"

He nodded. "You mustn't put yourself down, Emily, I'm sure you're often listened to."

She grimaced. "You know exactly my meaning. It was *you* I was getting at. You live in your own world and I didn't think I had a hope in hell of getting through."

"Well, you have."

"So, what exactly were my words of wisdom?"

"Something about treasures—guarding treasures."

Alessandro swilled the pale golden wine around the glass and looked at her from underneath guarded lids as she sighed with pleasure, savoring a mouthful of food. A vision of his wife, Eva, sitting back smoking as she eyed the dinner table with distaste, simply waiting for it to be over, entered his mind.

The contrast couldn't have been greater.

Avoiding Emily hadn't worked. She'd not left his mind, although he'd done his best to forget her.

But whether at work or at play he was confronted with women like Eva—self-absorbed, brittle and boring—and his mind turned once more to Emily.

Even when he was going out with women, flirting until it

was time to make love to them, he lost interest. His body wanted release, but not with them. He wanted only one woman. He'd never wanted only one woman and that was the dangerous part; that was the painful part. He couldn't risk it.

And he wouldn't have, if she hadn't turned up at his office today, showing the one trait that twisted the knife deeper inside him: vulnerability.

It disarmed him and suspended his judgment.

The feelings and thoughts that he'd suppressed during the week had surfaced and all he could think of was that she was, indeed, a treasure—just as he'd first thought—and that she needed guarding just as much as the archaeological site.

He refilled his glass and relaxed back in his seat once more. There was something joyous about watching someone relish their food. Nothing greedy, no hurried eating, but a savoring and a total absorption and appreciation of the culinary arts. It was very sensual. It was very arousing.

He must have conveyed something of his thoughts for she suddenly caught his eye and sat back, wary.

"So you're also here to guard the treasures."

He nodded. "You were correct. I have guards around the estate but no-one in the villa. It is safer to have someone here also."

She looked down, as if disappointed. He wouldn't enlighten her. He needed to be here for her, to make sure she was safe but that was all. The rest he would have to resist.

"It's a big villa."

He smiled. "You will be safe, believe me." He wouldn't tell her that he'd had his things moved to the room beside hers. She'd find out soon enough.

"Tell me, why did you tell the media about the dig? You must have known what would happen."

"I told you. Call it good business practice, if you will."

"I wouldn't."

"Then call it what you like."

"You could have ruined everything."

"Nonsense. If your reputation is as secure as you say, you will have no concerns. I have a business to run and publicity is a part of it."

"Business? What has the estate got to do with business?"

"The money you're using on the dig. The wages you're paying. Where do you think it comes from? Plucked out of the rarefied air of artistic academic sensibility? No. It comes from my businesses. Everything I own has to pay its way. Make me money."

"Why could publicity for the estate possibly benefit?"

"There is no such thing as bad publicity," he said evasively.

"You can't sell the antiquities you know."

"Thank you for enlightening me."

"So, your current project is?"

"I have a number of them. The largest is the redevelopment of a run-down area in Napoli that has great potential."

She sat back and looked at him. She'd taken her glasses off now and her green eyes seemed to burrow disconcertingly into him.

"You enjoy your work?"

"It's work. It has its challenges—and rewards." He shrugged.

"By rewards, you mean monetary."

"Not only money. Creating something out of nothing is satisfying."

"But it doesn't excite you, does it? There's no spark when you talk about it."

He narrowed his eyes. He wasn't used to being interrogated. "I thought you said I was the psychoanalyst."

She laughed. "Doesn't take a psychoanalyst to see you live for your pleasure time, not your work."

"Don't presume you can read me, Emily. The *past* is your area of expertise, not me."

Undaunted, Emily continued. "Now me, I love my work."

"Well, *cara*, we are not all so lucky."

"What's stopping you?"

"Enough, woman."

She grinned. "So your current project. Involves demolition first I guess?"

"We have to clear the area before we can build. The tenements in Forcella were razed to the ground before we could begin."

"You've 'razed it to the ground'? Now, that's not a phrase you often hear archaeologists say. In fact that's something you usually hear them use to describe the damage and desecration of a once unique civilization."

Her voice had become heated and Alessandro relaxed once more. Anger and argument he could deal with, sympathetic career advice, he couldn't.

"You think everything is so valuable it should be saved? The area we're developing has been a huddle of near derelict buildings of no use to anyone. Not everything needs to be saved."

"Perhaps you do though."

Her words fell like a heavy weight between them, redolent with meaning.

She'd gone too far. He pushed his chair back in sharp response. What the hell was she talking about?

"Now, if you've quite finished your interrogation, I'll leave you to your dinner. I have more of my destructive work to do. Goodnight."

"Alessandro?" Her quiet voice stopped him at the door.

He turned around slowly. "Thank you for coming back earlier. I appreciate it."

He nodded and continued out the door.

She drove him mad. One minute frustrating and angering him with her outspoken, almost naïve thoughts, and yet at other times her soft-spoken frankness could take his breath away with its simplicity.

But why the hell she should think he should be saved was beyond him. He had everything he wanted. Didn't he?

He walked down the marble corridor to the bedroom wing listening to the empty echo of his lonely footsteps and feeling, once more, the sharp pain of his guilt. He wondered why it was only when he was near Emily that his pain surfaced. He closed his eyes briefly, willing it to disappear but his mind was filled with the anxious face of his young son—floppy dark hair over a pale face that was inherited from Eva. A son who was no longer alive, thanks to him.

IT WAS late by the time Emily climbed the cool, sweep of stairs to the first floor rooms. The villa had a different atmosphere tonight. Not one to be easily spooked, she'd happily stayed here alone before Alessandro arrived. But now? She felt a tension in the air she hadn't noticed before.

She closed the door quietly behind her and turned on the gas lamps. They cast an eerie blue-white light in two pools, outside of which the darkness lay more thickly than before. The room was large and bare. She'd brought few personal possessions with her; she owned little, she needed even less. But tonight, somehow, she wished she'd made more of an imprint on the otherness of the room; she wished she could have claimed greater ownership. Perhaps then she'd have felt less threatened.

She moved over to the dark window and unfolded the

wooden shutters. They squeaked with disuse and refused to budge. With both hands she yanked at each of the shutters in turn, growing more desperate to shut out the blind darkness that lay outside.

Then she saw it.

A slight movement of something pale below her window. Her eyes burned as she stared, unblinking, into the darkness. But all she could see was a trail of twitching branches through a sea of unmoving darkness. She opened her mouth to cry out, but no sound came. She couldn't move. She stood transfixed as her eyes adjusted to the night, now seeing layers of darkness, different textures, a movement of the tree tops in the light, night breeze.

Again she saw it: a light flash of a lone torch tracking its way through the bushes from the rear of the house. Still she couldn't move. Then she heard the crisp snap of a branch directly beneath her window.

She backed away slowly as though the person might detect her movements. Her shadow, doubled from each of the two lights, twisted away from her, up the walls and cast its darkness onto the ceiling.

Anyone from outside could see her now.

A beam of torchlight turned suddenly up on to the window before dropping down.

She cried out loud, involuntarily, and lunged at the door, twisted the handle and rushed out into the black corridor, straight into the body of a man, naked except for a towel around his middle.

She cried out again, more loudly this time, and pulled away, but hands held her tight.

"Stop, Emily, it's only me." Alessandro pulled her more firmly to him. She could feel the steady thud of his heart against her ear as she tried to stay the panic that still filled her.

"Alessandro! There's someone outside. A torch, shining into my room."

"Hush. It's only the guards. Come, I'll show you." He took her back into her room and went to the opened window. "See?" He called down and a guard emerged from the shadows. "È tutto ok?"

"Si, signore."

"Andare aventi."

She heard the guard leave but he still held her trembling body in his arms and he gently sat her down on the bed before going back over the window and pulling the shutters closed with a firm tug.

He poured her a glass of water.

"I'm sorry you were alarmed."

"I feel stupid. You told me about the guards. They just slipped my mind and when I saw the movements, I thought —" She stopped abruptly.

"What did you think?"

She shook her head. Then looked up at him. "Why were you outside my room?"

"I've moved rooms and I heard you cry out."

"You've moved rooms?"

"Yes, I thought it best."

"Best? For whom?"

He put down the glass of water abruptly, spilling a few drops. "You made it quite clear in the office that you were worried. And, after what just happened, I can see you're nervous. I've changed rooms because you asked for protection. I'm here to give it. At night at least."

"Yes, I'm sorry. It's just that I'm not used to being looked after. I guess I'm a bit cynical about such offers."

"Cynicism in one so young? I wonder why?" His voice dropped. "Emily, I'm just here to keep you safe."

She knew it. She felt it. His presence changed her room and she did feel safe. But she felt something more.

He stood close, too close. She felt out of kilter, unreal. She couldn't think straight.

"Safe?" she repeated.

"Yes. Safe." He sat beside her and put his arm around her and drew her into the warmth and protection of his body. "Safe from the phantom that haunts you."

She closed her eyes tight as she drew a long, deep breath into her lungs. She did feel safe, safe enough to allow the image of her ex-boyfriend to enter her mind. Because he was her only phantom.

"How do you know about him?"

She felt his grip tighten in response to her words.

"Him?" A different note had crept into his tone—confusion, suspicion, of hurt even. It brought her back to her senses.

Phantom? He couldn't possibly know. He was simply referring to her vague fears of archaeological sabotage.

She pulled away from him reluctantly.

"I— I'm sorry." Her head began to pound. "That's right. I'm worried about people who will stop at nothing to take away a piece of what doesn't belong to them."

He couldn't know that she was still talking about her ex.

"No-one will get to you, here, Emily. I guarantee it. Whoever it is you are scared of."

Somehow his arms had come around her again, tentatively this time, and drawn her close to him.

This time she stayed close, not because of fear, but because this was the place she wanted to be. She felt, for the first time ever, that she was truly safe. As though she'd come home.

She could feel his cheek rest gently on her head in an intimate gesture that was far more devastating to her than any kiss could have been. She breathed his body in slowly and then pulled away and looked up into his eyes. They were shadowed in the darkness, but she could feel their intensity upon her.

He cupped her face with his hands.

"*Cara*. I don't know what is going on in that head of yours. I know nothing about you. But I do know one thing, I want to know you more. For the moment, you need me. And that is all I have to offer. The moment. Would you be happy with that?"

She nodded, unable to break the spell of her body and mind in this man's arms.

"Don't leave me."

Her voice was a whisper.

CHAPTER 5

*S*he awoke to find him gone.

The pale grey light of early dawn was fingering its way through the old shutters onto the bare boards of her room, illuminating the rich colors of the Persian rug and revealing the empty bed beside her.

Tentatively she spread her fingers over the sheets. They were still warm. He hadn't broken his word.

She rose and eased open the stiff shutters.

The morning was forming out of the early dawn darkness. The air was moist and fragrant and absolutely still. No gentle breeze playing, no movement of foliage, just a heavy, quiet, calm. She narrowed her eyes, assessingly.

It felt like change was in the air. But what? Before Emily could identify the source of her unease the door swung open behind her.

Alessandro entered, showered and dressed, looking like he'd just stepped out of Italian Vogue. She swallowed. Could she really have been held by this man all night? He was out of her league. She knew it, why didn't he?

She pulled the tie around her dressing gown more tightly.

She hoped he'd keep his distance.

"How are you this morning, Emily? Shaken away the shadows yet?"

Any resistance melted at the concern on his face.

She hoped he'd come close. She shook her head at her contradictory thoughts and turned away.

He smiled as if in response to her expression, walked around to face her and brushed the back of his fingers down her cheek.

"Well?"

She willed herself to focus on his question, not on the heat that his hands sent traversing through her face, through her nerve endings, lighting up every part of her.

"The shadows? They're gone. For now. Look, thanks. Thanks for being with me. I was being stupid—I don't know what got into me. But thanks for being there for me."

"My pleasure." There was something in his tone that didn't make her doubt his sincerity.

Her heart was beating fast. Just the smell of him, the nearness of him, the texture of his fingers on her skin was driving her to distraction. If she didn't get away now she'd make a huge fool of herself and throw herself on him. And she didn't want to start the day by being a laughing stock. Which is what she'd be because what could a beautiful Italian billionaire possibly want with her?

She smiled briefly, awkwardly and glanced around, anywhere but at him.

"Anyway, I'd better get ready for the day." She stepped away but his hands simply fell to her shoulders and stayed there. She couldn't find the strength to move further from his arms.

"You're not working today."

"I always work on a Saturday."

"No, Emily, I have other plans for us. A surprise."

She felt a sense of panic. "What plans? I don't like surprises. I need to know."

"It wouldn't be a surprise then would it?"

She couldn't fault his logic. And she couldn't argue with him after he stayed with her last night: chastely, only holding, not asking, not wanting anything more. "OK. But why? What's all this about?"

"I want to get to know you better, away from all these ancient things, this old world. You spend too much time in the past. You need to get away—with me."

She felt a shiver run down her spine. "Sounds interesting."

"But first, we will go shopping."

She grimaced. "Sounds horrific."

"Don't worry. I will make it as painless as possible. I have people working on it."

"How can they know what to buy?"

"Because, *cara*, I have told them. They will leave the final selection to me."

"I don't understand. Why do you want to do this? Are you trying to make me into someone else? Is that it?"

"Emily! Why would I want to do that?"

"No idea."

"Who do you imagine I would want you to look like?"

She shrugged. "Just someone you'd want to be around."

"I want to be around you." His hands gripped her shoulders more tightly before dropping down and caressing her arms and back. She winced, knowing that he was touching the very scars that prevented them from being together. Because once he found out he'd realize what she knew already, that she wasn't of his world.

She shook her head, her heart too full to speak.

"*Cara*, why do you not believe me? I thought I made it plain last night." He sighed and let her go, his hands brushing down the sides of her body, his eyes taking in the bulky lines of the toweling robe that had seen better days. He looked into her eyes, all irritation gone, replaced by a spark of humor. "But I would also like to look at you in something other than those rags you call clothes and those glasses which must be the most unattractive I've ever seen."

"There's nothing wrong with my glasses."

"And that, Emily, is why you need help."

"Anyway, clothes don't matter to me."

"Then it won't matter to you if I buy you a new wardrobe, will it? Come, you're wasting time. The staff has laid out an early breakfast for us. And then we will leave."

EMILY LOOKED out the window of the private jet and wondered where she'd missed his reference to flying.

Below her, Naples tumbled down to the water that sparkled in the morning sunlight. Perched on the hill the fortress of Castel Sant'Elmo watched over the old city with its blend of old and new, of poor and rich that gave the city its vibrancy, its edge. Other cities may be more beautiful, more cosmopolitan, more sophisticated but none could compete with its passionate personality and sense of danger.

She turned to look at Alessandro. He was sipping an espresso as he checked his emails. Her heart thudded. What was she doing with this gorgeous creature, as dangerous as the city from which he came?

He was, as usual, dressed in clothes that even she could tell were of the finest fabrics and cut, taut across his back and shoulders where he leaned forward over his laptop, and loosely skimming his muscled chest and stomach. But any sense of vanity was dissipated by how he wore them: shirt, open at the neck, one sleeve pushed up and the other folded twice. And his hair, as usual, managed to be sexily tousled without being unkempt. How did he do it?

She had the careless thing going but obviously managed to look like someone who needed sorting out. Irritated, she returned her gaze to the window.

"So, where are we going?"

He looked up at her and grinned. "Still a surprise."

"What is it with you and surprises?" she grumbled. She picked up a briosce and took a big bite. "Surprises make me hungry."

He laughed. "Everything makes you hungry. I'd hate to see you after you've worked up an appetite." His eyes narrowed. "In fact, I'd rather watch you work up an appetite." He snapped the laptop shut.

She glanced at him and frowned. "I'm glad I don't know what you're talking about." She flicked a look at her watch. "I could be getting on with work now."

"All work and no play, makes Emily a dull girl. I think that is your English expression?"

"Something like that. Not that anyone's said it to me before."

"Poor Emily. No-one has wanted to play with you before?"

She looked down before he could see that his jibe had been less playful than he'd intended.

She shook her head and looked up at him once more, having regained her composure. "Alessandro. I don't know if anyone has told you, but you are very bad news."

"Strange you should say this, because they have. What can I say? I like to play. I like to follow my nose and see where it goes. Surely you must have done that."

"With work, of course. I follow leads, hunches, but with work. Play is that small amount of time between eating and bed. Usually about half an hour when I catch up with my reading."

He rose and stood over her. "You, *cara*, are a sad person."

"Is that right?"

"It is. And I fully intend to do something about it."

"How would you know what would make me happy?"

As soon as the words slipped out she could have bitten her tongue. By the look on his face—an expression of indecent carnal knowledge—she could see that he knew exactly how to make her happy.

"I have a few ideas and I'll try them, one by one, until I find the one that works."

She couldn't look away and he refused to. Then he smiled and glanced over her shoulder, out of the window.

"We're nearly there."

"Where?"

"Milan, of course. Where else to buy clothes?"

"If you think that's going to make me happy, you're wrong."

"I am under no such illusion. Shopping for clothes for you, is in order to make *me* happy."

EMILY PUSHED her new shoes off and wriggled her toes. It wasn't that they were uncomfortable. It was that she'd never worn shoes that were *so* comfortable. It was as if they weren't there. She slipped her feet back inside, relishing the caress of the soft leather. She sat back from the table of the exclusive restaurant and crossed her legs, flexing her foot first one way and then another so she could see them from different angles.

"So, Emily, I take it that you approve of the shoes at least?"

She looked up, startled out of her reverie, and grinned. "They're OK."

He laughed. And she wanted to hold that picture of him in her mind forever. The dark, pine-clad mountains surrounding the brilliant azure of Lake Como, provided a fitting backdrop of beauty to his own but did not eclipse it. She took a sip of wine.

"Just OK?"

She broadened her smile. "They're fantastic. Thank you."

"My pleasure."

"And mine." She lowered her eyelashes, surreptitiously eyeing her shoes briefly before looking up at him, attitude firmly in place once more. "But you really didn't need me there, did you? You knew exactly what you wanted and it wouldn't have mattered if I said 'no'."

"But you didn't."

"Didn't see the point of trying to stop an Italian in full flight. Pointless exercise."

"But you like the clothes."

She brushed her hand down the silky fabric of the dress and wriggled her feet back into the shoes again. "They are gorgeous. But I would never have picked them for me in a million years."

"Because you have no taste. But, admit it, you enjoyed shopping didn't you?"

She assumed an expression of mock seriousness. "I will never admit that. It would be bad for my reputation."

"I'd like to hear more about your reputation."

"Well, I'm thorough and know my stuff but it isn't that that earned me my reputation as a scholar.

"Then what was it?"

"Imagination. You had to have imagination. To make the links, you see."

"I like imagination in a woman." He sipped his wine and looked lazily over the table at Emily. "And thoroughness. Si. A good combination."

Her eyes slid from his gaze and she could feel a wave of

heat, that had nothing to do with the hot sun, rise through her body.

In an effort to divert her thoughts she took a mouthful of the freshly-caught lavarelli served in an exquisitely green, piquant sauce.

"It's good?" Alessandro still hadn't eaten anything.

"Yes, you should try it."

"It's more fun watching you eat."

She let her fork drop with a clatter on to the plate. "I think I've had enough."

"Come. Don't let an audience put you off."

"No. It's your clothes I blame because you can practically see what I ate for breakfast. Look at this." She sucked in her tummy and ran her hands around her hips where the fabric draped seductively. She forgot that the pulling in of her stomach made her breasts push out even further.

"Umm. I'm looking."

She looked up at him and caught him grinning as his gaze lingered on her cleavage.

"Very, very bad news. Have I told you that?"

He laughed. "Then why are you here with me?"

"I don't know." She put down her glass of wine. "I've been asking myself the same question."

"And have you come up with any answers?"

"No, only another question. Why did you ask me to come with you? You could be with anyone."

He shook his head in confusion. "I don't understand you. Why do you think so little of yourself that you would doubt I would want to be with you? You're beautiful. I've never met anyone like you before. You are your own person: strong-willed, you know who you are. That, Emily, is incredibly sexy."

"Then you're the first to notice," she muttered in embarrassment.

"Your English boyfriends must have been blind."

She didn't like to correct the plural. She didn't like him talking about her romantic past at all. Not that there had been much romance.

"So, you've always been surrounded by women who don't know who they are? They must be easy to confuse."

He put his head to one side and narrowed his eyes. "How so?"

"All you need to say is: 'who are you?' Got them in one."

He laughed. "And your sense of humor, for another. Very rare in my circles."

"Circles are bad. Just make you go round and round. Just as well your father set you on a different trajectory."

"It set me on course to you."

All amusement had vanished, replaced by a quiet tension in his voice and a darkening of his eyes that sent shivers down her spine. It told of a strength of feeling that simmered beneath the surface, out of sight, but powerful nevertheless.

Emily gulped her wine down and stared across the lake to the wooded hills beyond.

"Alessandro. Stop it."

"What?"

"You're staring at me."

"It's because I want to kiss you."

She swallowed and could feel his eyes watching every shift of her throat.

"What's your favorite music?"

"What?"

"I'm trying to distract you. Your favorite music."

"If you must know, I love all good music: classical, jazz—"

She caught his eyes. "Civilized, laid back."

"OK, what's your favorite type of music?"

"Country and Western."

He laughed. "Of course. It's the stories you like."

"You got it."

He sat forward and picked up his cutlery. "So, if I promise not to flirt with you during the serious business of eating, will you eat also?"

"It's a deal."

Alessandro could hardly keep his eyes off her. Her conversation was always lively but he could scarcely concentrate. Her blond, sun-streaked hair shivered around her sun-tanned arms. The dress, while having a deep neckline, covered her shoulders. He knew about her scars but she always kept them covered and he didn't want to make her uncomfortable. On the contrary, he wanted her very comfortable. His eyes fell to her breasts: barely concealed by the soft fabric. They were full, round and it was all he could do not to reach over and run his finger around their outer point, to watch them peak with desire.

That was what he wanted. And that was what he was going to get.

His eyes dropped lower still to her slightly rounded stomach—so sensuous, he wanted to cup it with his hand—down to her legs, long and lean. It was a crime to cover them in the boyish shorts and jeans she normally wore. The low heels—he thought high ones would be pushing his luck—didn't scream femme fatale, but were softly feminine. He particularly liked the way she slipped them off periodically and rubbed each arch with the opposite foot as if seeking reassurance that they were OK in these alien shoes.

Funny, how a body talked so much more meaningfully than words.

"You haven't heard a word I've been saying."

He looked up at her green eyes—paler in the bright sunshine but just as intriguing—and smiled. "No. I've been admiring you."

A cloud seemed to lower over her expression.

"There's nothing to admire. Stop it, Alessandro, this—this charade. What is it all about—all this dressing me up in clothes of your choosing—control? You want to prove your manliness by controlling me? That's what men do isn't it?"

He frowned, trying to understand her sudden turn of mood. "*Cara*, calm down. I am not after anything. I have enough in my life that I can control. I don't need anything more. I simply wish to admire. Not take anything you're not willing to give."

He saw her almost deflate with his words.

"I'm sorry. It's just that I'm not used to this. I don't want anything more than what I have. And I think you do. What is it you want, Alessandro? What is it you think you've just bought?"

"I'd hoped I'd just brought—not bought—you and me some pleasure. Was I wrong?"

She shook her head. "I'm not a pleasure-seeking kind of woman."

"No. You're a stubborn one."

"Stubborn is good."

"Possibly. But not easy."

"You'd be bored with easy."

He smiled then. "And you don't want me to be bored do you?"

She grimaced, realizing that she'd just given away her true feelings.

"No. I don't want to bore you."

"Why?"

"Because I enjoy your company."

"Did that hurt so much to say?"

She lowered her eyes and nodded. "A little."

"And I enjoy yours." He raised his glass. "A toast. To pleasure."

She hesitated but couldn't resist the look in his eyes.

When she finally looked away she realized that she was sunk. She'd fallen for him and there was no getting away from it this time.

BY THE TIME they returned it was nearly midnight. The guards were in place and Emily felt more light-headed than she'd felt for years as they walked up to the villa, Alessandro's arm resting lightly around her shoulders.

She waited as Alessandro spoke briefly to the guards.

"What did you say?"

"I told them to concentrate on the dig site from now on. I'll look after the villa."

He drew out a chair for her on the terrazza overlooking the wide lawn and the rambling garden beyond.

"Sit, I will get us some wine."

She sank down into the soft cushions and ran her hands down her dress and wriggled her feet out of her shoes for the hundredth time. She'd never imagined that she would wear such things. They made her feel a different woman. They made her feel—

She bit her lip and looked into the dark distance.

She couldn't fool herself into believing how they made her feel. They didn't change things.

But the brief veil of sadness couldn't shift the magic of the night. The stars were brilliant in the sky, the weather still unnaturally calm. Waiting weather. The memory of this morning's awareness that change was coming flitted through her mind. But again Alessandro disturbed it.

He placed the glasses and bottle of wine on the table and sat beside her. He put his arm around her and pulled her to him.

"It's beautiful here. I can't believe you'd ever want to leave it."

She felt his arm stiffen. "I don't stay anywhere for long. I am only here now because of my father's will."

"Why did he make that request of you, Alessandro?"

He shrugged. "I don't know. I have my suspicions. He was a deep man, a scholar, a thinker. I think he wanted me to stop."

"Stop? What?"

"Everything." He turned so he could see her. "But I'm not interested in talking about my father, or me, tonight."

"What are you interested in talking about?"

"You, of course."

"Ah, of course. Well, what can I say? I hardly know myself any more. I feel so different."

"And why is that?"

"Come on. Don't I look different?"

He tilted his head to one side and considered her. "A little. We didn't go shopping for you to look or feel different, Emily. It is you I'm interested in, not someone else, not some created person."

"I'm glad. I mean, I wondered what you were trying to do, whether you were trying to create a perfect person."

She couldn't help her voice faltering on the word "perfect".

He picked up her hand and kissed it gently.

"You're trembling."

"You're close."

"What would you do if I were closer?"

"Tremble some more."

"I'd better test that."

He stood up and raised her to her feet, put his arms gently around her and kissed her softly.

Contradictory sensations flooded her body: her heart hammered and heat filled her, and yet time seemed to slow as she felt his tongue slide against hers and her body press to his—the sensations felt fully with each pressure point, each hot trail left by his hand, experienced minutely.

She shifted more closely to him, her arms wrapping around him, her feverish hands caressing places that she'd been wanting to touch ever since they'd met. Slowly her thoughts slipped away, overwhelmed by the myriad sensations her fingers brought to her mind.

He pulled away. "Not much trembling there. You seem to have overcome your nerves."

"I think I've overcome everything, including thinking."

His eyes roamed her face, drinking in every detail. She felt suddenly distanced. She didn't want him to see every detail of her. Because she didn't want him to be disgusted. And he would be, this appreciator of everything perfect.

But then he kissed her again and swept all thoughts away once more.

"Come, *cara*, let's go inside. I've dismissed the guards from around the house but I still don't wish our pleasure to be observed."

Dream-like she followed the tug of his hand as he led her inside and up the flight of stairs to the other wing of the house.

He unlocked a room and took her inside.

She'd not been in any of the locked rooms before and was transfixed. Medieval in origin the plaster walls in this wing were still decorated with the original medieval paintings. Soft ochre faded into the gentlest of autumn reds and yellows and the palest grey-green. The spread wings of the Archangel Gabriel was presumably designed to give the sleeper shelter at night. Now, with the passing years, the outline was indistinct and not so awe-inspiring as it must once have been.

"Wow! You've been keeping something from me."

"I hope you have the same response in a few moments."

She laughed and walked up to the painting. Her fingers hovered over its beauty, not wanting to touch and add to the painting's deterioration but desperately wanting to commune with something so beautiful.

She hadn't heard him approach but felt his hands on her shoulders, gently caressing. She closed her eyes. If only he knew what lay beneath the exquisite dress.

How could she go through with this? It couldn't go anywhere, not when he knew. She didn't think she could bear the inevitable look of disgust on his face. She felt his warm lips upon her neck, sending shivers of sensation down her back, heating her body and freezing any thoughts of hesitancy.

She turned in his arms and their lips met with a heat and urgency that had been latent during the day. His hands covered her back and slid around to her waist and hips, smoothly over the fine fabric.

She'd waited a long time to explore with her hands where her mind had been every time she'd been with him. Now, she could feel the tight muscles under his shirt. But it wasn't enough. She pushed up the fabric of his shirt and felt the heated skin beneath. Her hands slid to his stomach where the muscles clenched.

"*Dio, cara*. But I want you."

She blinked under the gas lamps. They brought her to reality and she stretched to turn them off.

"But I want to see you."

"No, no you don't."

He let her slide away and she extinguished the lights. The room was completely dark now, with no moon, and no neighboring lights to expose her.

He reached over and guided her to him.

This time his lips lowered to her neck, her breasts and then his hands slid to the top of the zip. In one movement the shimmering fabric fell to the ground. Even in the darkness, Emily felt suddenly nervous, exposed. But his lips made her fears disappear under the lust they ignited.

He didn't touch her body with his hands, other than to undo her bra and pull down her panties. His hands then went into her hair, bunching it up as he pulled her face to his.

"I want to see you."

"No lights."

"Then I must feel you and taste you."

She could hardly stop shaking. Her breathing came quickly, she was instantly moist at his words.

He kissed her again, savoring and exploring, not taking. His kiss was like a connoisseur's enjoyment: intellectually enjoying, but in control. His finger trailed down her chest and toyed with her nipples that were hard and grew harder. But his touch was too playful. She wanted more. She pressed herself against him.

But he drew away and she heard his soft chuckle as his hands lowered and his palm cupped her stomach.

"I've been longing to do this. Do you know how sensual your stomach is? Its curve just fits my hands and," his fingers turned and lowered, "it's like an appetizer before the main course." She gasped as his fingers explored her. But then he withdrew and led her to the bed.

"Please. Alessandro." She tried to undo his shirt.

"No. Not yet. Don't be impatient. I'm not finished with you yet."

He laid her down on the bed and his hands swept up her legs, her hips, her stomach and caressed her breasts.

She groaned and he responded by shifting his mouth to where his hands had been.

Shocked, she arched her back as his lips and teeth played with her, drawing her out. She'd never felt such pleasure: it flowed from her breasts along a direct link to that part of her that, even now, shivered with anticipation.

For once she took pleasure in the size of her breasts, normally so inconvenient that she hid them under baggy shirts. She could feel his appreciation and it made her enjoy her own sexuality. She felt more confident. She pushed her hands through his hair, closing her eyes, allowing the sensations to wash over her in increasing intensity. She gasped as each wave of sensation increased. She opened her legs to allow him closer access, wanting him to be not close but a part of her now.

But still he held back. He released her breasts with a lingering caress and stood up.

Her eyes had become accustomed to the dark and the distant lights of far-off Naples gave a contrast to the dark, so slight, but enough to see his shadow as he smoothly slid out of his clothes.

She sat up and reached out for him.

Her hands slipped around his back and she drew him down on top of her. His body was hot against hers and their lips met as she felt his leg between hers. She curled her leg around him as their bodies pressed hard against each other and they rolled onto their side.

Emily had only one thing driving her. She needed to feel his body—so much larger than her own—hard against her and inside her. There was no time for enjoyment, for savoring; she wanted only one thing. To have him drive into her and take her away from herself—make her forget herself in her physical need for him, a need so powerful that there was nothing else at that moment.

She twisted and turned in his arms—her mounting need almost becoming a panic—and within moments was sitting astride his thighs. She wriggled forward so she could feel his body pressing against her. Then she held him in both hands and closed her eyes, focusing on the feel of him as she wriggled lightly against him while holding his erection in her hands. She stroked, tentative at first, with her fingers before encircling him with her hands. Unable to wait another moment, she gasped, and felt the length of him against herself before she slipped over and down, sinking, trembling onto him, slowly, slowly, her body wracked with sensation with each slight movement down, her wetness easing his size, the tension building inside with each tiny slide. When she reached the bottom of his shaft, she cried aloud into the dark night.

"*Cara*," he pulled her down and eased her around until she was under him, his body sheltering hers. He eased out of her then.

"No!" Her cry was urgent, desperate.

"I need to protect you *cara*."

Within moments he was back inside her, where he belonged. In that one entry she'd felt herself move to fit him, take on his shape, educate her body that this was the man who should be there. So when he slipped back into her, she wriggled her hips in pleasure at the welcome return of something that needed to be there. She knew in that moment, that she'd always want him—would be waiting until his return to her when he could enter her and she would be complete once more.

He moved himself carefully inside her again and she raised her hips to take him fully. With her first needs met, she could take the time to feel him now. His body strained with control, anticipation. She rubbed the soles of her feet against his calves, relishing the feel of her thighs around his hips, as they slipped forward and back, once more building up the coils of tension that spiraled within.

She pulled him tight against her with her legs. Suddenly a light was turned on far away, dim, but enough so that they could see each other's eyes. Their gaze held for a long moment during which neither moved. Their intimate physical connection mirrored something more intense that was savored—suspending movement and thought—until finally their bodies regained control and he gave her what she wanted. There were no loud cries this time. Their eyes still held each other until their lips came together and stifled their cries of ecstasy.

EMILY WATCHED as the light changed imperceptibly, darkening and deepening with the coming of dawn. She closed her eyes and felt his presence. She didn't have to see him to be filled with a sense of him that she knew would never leave; she could taste him on her lips, she could smell him, see him, feel him still.

She turned instinctively towards him as she heard him stir. She tensed as his hand slid towards her, searching for her body. She shifted her hand between them and he covered it with his. He relaxed again then, and soon his breathing once more settled into a rhythmic pattern that seemed to be her own. Her other hand hovered over his chest, wanting to touch him, as it rose with each breath taken.

She didn't have much time. The light was creeping in, throwing a gauzy haze across the room's darkness, creating shapes where none had existed before. She'd have to move before he awoke. She couldn't let him see her for what she was. For several precious minutes, she watched his pulse, flicking at his neck with each beat of his heart.

She'd found the man who was her home—the place she wanted to be—the family she'd never had. But what about him? Was she the family he was looking for?

She knew the answer and lay back on the pillow, looking up at the beautiful, moulded ceiling, as intricate and delicate as a wedding cake. It was a vision of beauty as everything else was in the room, including him. The thought of his disappointment and disgust when he saw her for what she really was, filled her with grief. She'd found the place she wanted to be, but she was worlds away from this man, poles apart, only together because of the wild notions of his father. And once their time was over? He'd be gone. Because she wasn't the perfect lover to keep him.

How long did she have?

She pulled her hand gently from under his and rolled quietly off the bed. She grabbed her clothes and left the room without a backward glance. She had no need to see him. She would never forget him, because he existed within her now, always.

CHAPTER 6

*E*mily couldn't help but smile to herself. It was too perfect: the snowy-white alps sparkling under the morning sun, rippling beneath the jet as they flew over north Italy, heading for who-knew-where.

"And what, Miss M, makes you smile?"

Alessandro handed her a glass of chilled champagne.

"It's so beautiful. Nothing has a right to be that beautiful."

"Not everyone sees the beauty in things."

She felt her smile slip as the reality of the sentence hit home. Not now. She wouldn't think of it now.

She lifted her chin and met his gaze. "Just as well too. Otherwise everybody would want the same thing."

"And what is it you want, Miss M? You claim to be a single-minded archaeologist. But I'm not so sure. What are you really digging for? I don't believe it's for the betterment of academics everywhere. There's a personal quality to it. There's something else that's driving you."

She smiled uncertainly and looked back at the Alps. "Not the gold you're digging for."

"A kind of gold, perhaps."

"Perhaps."

"So evasive, so secret."

"As are you. You haven't told me where we're going to yet. Where to this time?" Emily grinned. "New York, Sydney, Beijing?"

"We have been lovers for less than a week and already you are demanding. You see, I told you that you would fit in."

"So you're not going to tell me. Another secret."

"No. I have had enough of secrets. Life with you needs no further excitement."

"Then where? I guess it's not far if we've to return to Naples this evening."

"Ah yes, my venerable father's legacy."

"Why did he do it? Why did he stipulate that you must also stay at the villa? Me, I can understand. But you?"

He sat back out of the rays of the harsh sun, his eyes now in shadow. He shrugged lightly. "Who knows? I'd been a way a long time. Perhaps he thought I needed to return."

"Return home?"

"Return to my past, maybe. But, yes, you're correct. We can't go far if we are to return to the villa tonight. We are going to Paris. It's a fund-raiser being organized by some friends. It should be fun."

"Are they expecting me?"

"Yes, of course. I told them I would be bringing a friend."

She raised her eyebrows in mock indignation but it was lost on Alessandro as he rose to talk to the pilot who'd just entered the cabin. It wasn't exactly how she'd hoped he'd describe her. Nevertheless she couldn't help smiling. He was incorrigible and in his element: chatting to the staff, answering business calls on his cell and flirting with her. The bon vivant doing what he did best.

How the hell did she get together with someone like him?

The past week had been perfect. She had never imagined

making love could be so intense, so exquisitely emotional. Sex with Marcus had been satisfying at first, giving her a closeness to someone she'd never before experienced. But that hadn't lasted long as he tried to exert control over her in the bedroom. And the worst of it was that she had nothing to compare it to; she'd thought it must be normal to have a domineering partner. The more successful she'd become at work, the more confident around people, the worse he'd become—subjecting her to his will by sheer brute force. But he'd always followed it up with apologies, lies about loving her, things that confused her into submission once more. Things, she later realized, that were simply ways of continuing to exert control over her.

He'd been a master at it, manipulating her until she didn't know what was true and what was false; what was love and what was hate. But she knew what pain was. And what pain meant.

Only then had it ended, long after it should have ended.

She'd never again looked for love, knowing that it didn't exist. She hated Marcus more than ever now, because he'd stopped her from seeking what she now knew to exist.

She loved Alessandro with all her heart and soul and body.

If only she could be right for him.

He finished his conversation and the crew returned to their quarters and Alessandro returned to his seat. Even if his height and broad shoulders hadn't filled the physical space with his presence, there was something about his manner— the way he moved, the way he looked—that was a clear signal to everyone that he was in charge. But not in the way that Marcus had always believed.

She shivered as he sat down beside her and turned to look at her closely, questioningly, his hand trailing slowly up her leg.

"You looked lost in your thoughts, Emily. Tell me what you were thinking about?"

"You can't expect me to think as you run your hand up my leg."

"Umm. That's tricky. Do I want your mind, in which case I should stop distracting you or do I want your body?"

"Better choose my mind. In case you hadn't noticed we're in a plane with people working just the other side of that door."

"True. It is a beautiful mind and an interesting mind—a rare combination—but one mustn't forget the body. It can have a profound effect on one's mind." His hand didn't stop moving up towards her thigh.

She clamped her hand on top of his. "It's having one on mine. It's telling me that we'll be landing soon. There's no time."

"We have half an hour yet before we land."

He pushed his hand further up her thigh and she felt her hand slip away from his, allowing him freer access. Her body melted under his touch, her mind ceased to function as she felt the soft drag of his nails climbing further up her inner thigh. She felt herself quiver with anticipation and longing.

She swallowed hard. The light was too bright up here. She just couldn't. Not yet.

"I've got, well, reading to do."

He laughed. "Reading? Are you mad?" He kissed her long and slow on her lips, his finger now sliding between the elastic of her panties and her super-sensitive skin.

She gasped. "Alessandro! Someone might come in."

"No, they won't. It would be more than their life or their job is worth. But we can go to the bedroom if you like. I'll take off your clothes one by one and make love to you under the brilliant sun of the Alps."

She shook her head. "No. I'll stay here if you don't—"

"That's fine with me." With one swift movement he yanked down her panties. "Don't move an inch. I promise not to rumple your beautiful new clothes." He flicked back her seat and she landed on her back on the cushions with a yelp, that turned into a sigh, that turned into a small cry of ecstasy that was drowned by the thrum of the jet as it flew high across Europe.

SHE TOOK a deep breath and smoothed down her jacket and skirt.

He dropped a kiss on her head as she bobbed down to enter the limo. "You see, not a wrinkle."

"You're an expert at this, obviously."

"Everyone has their talents, *cara*, what can I say?"

"Nothing. Actions speak louder than words."

He took her hand and squeezed it in a demonstration of affection and warmth that thrilled her. There was something in the familiarity of the gesture that made her very happy. She looked out the window at Paris: soft, grey, drizzly and impossibly beautiful. She'd been there only once before and had loved it instantly.

"First stop, the hotel bedroom." His whisper tickled her ear. He turned to instruct the driver but Emily put a hand on his arm and pressed the intercom instead.

"Musee d'Orsay." She turned to Alessandro. "Please. It's years since I've been."

He sighed. "You'll simply have to make up for lost time later Miss M." He turned to the driver. "Musee d'Orsay."

EMILY KNEW EXACTLY where she wanted to go. She drew Alessandro on, beyond the immaculate sculptures, beyond the huge scale of Monet's paintings and the blistering impact of the Picassos, to a dimly lit corner of the museum.

There she stopped and felt the atmosphere take her back, back to her early days of convalescence when she'd come here and first seen the Lautrecs.

Would it be here? Her favourite picture, the one that spoke to her the most. It wasn't always on display. But today?

"Ah. So it's Toulouse Lautrec who has captured your heart."

"Everything is wonderful in here but there's something about these that get to me." She stood in front of the painting for which she'd been searching. "Look." She must have conveyed something of the awe she felt because he didn't look at the painting first, but at her. Then he turned to the painting.

"The colors are extraordinary."

"Greys, mauves, pale golds and then there's her red hair. Apparently he liked redheads best. And it's, well, just ordinary. An ordinary scene—La Toilette—but made extraordinary. He's not doing the 'I'm a great artist and painting this masterpiece' thing. He's there, in it, like he *is* that woman, he feels for her so." She stepped away from the picture as she felt her emotions beginning to run away with her. "I don't know. Silly really."

"Not silly at all." He pulled her close to him, his arm tight around her as they both stood in front of the painting.

"It's there, in everything, even in the hatching of the crayons or oils or whatever he used. It's an empathy with the subject. He's not trying to own it, do something to it, just to reveal it. Don't look at me like that. I don't know anything about paintings. Just," her hand hovered, "it's so moving. And he's not even showing her face."

"No, he has no need. Her bare back shows everything—a

slight tension in the shoulders coming down to a sensuously soft middle and soft, creamy skin—beautiful."

"Flawless." She pulled her light coat around her, tying the belt more tightly.

"You're pale, *cara*. Come." He took her by the hand and pulled her out onto the balcony. She took a deep breath and absorbed the display of Parisian rooftops all around them. She could be nowhere else but Paris.

"I liked the way the artist was looking at her." She looked up at him. "He wasn't trying to own her, to control her. He wouldn't have hurt her would he?"

He shook his head, his brows contracting slightly as if in puzzlement, and then pulled her tight to him.

"Come. We should get to the hotel now. We don't have much time."

"Sure."

He hadn't got it. He didn't understand.

HE WAS RIGHT. By the time they reached the hotel, showered and changed they were back out again, walking down through the Marais district with its grand medieval and seventeenth-century buildings.

The rain had cleared and they walked, hand in hand, down the leafy streets, cars speeding by, beautiful people venturing out for the evening. And for once in her life, Emily felt a deep sense of happiness.

He might never understand her fully. But why should he? His experiences were so totally different to hers. But here, now, with this man, she had everything she wanted.

"You're happy, I think."

She nodded, unable to let herself speak for fear of tearing up.

"Good. I want you always to be happy, mio tesoro."

"'Always' is a big ask; 'now', is fine."

He laughed. "You're even beginning to sound like me. *For now. For the present.*"

She cast him a quick glance. There was an edge to his last few words that made her wonder. He pushed open a creaking wrought-iron gate and pulled her into a deserted garden square. Behind the barrier of trees and walls, the sounds of the street faded. It was just them.

"Tell me, Emily. Is that enough for you. Truthfully?"

The moon had risen over the tall buildings and showered them both with silvered light. Dark, light. All, nothing. It was always extremes. She had been used to nothing all her life. And with Alessandro she had found happiness—a happiness that had no future because Alessandro wanted it that way. How could she possibly want anything more? But she did.

Did he want her to agree with him, say that now was enough? Or did he want the truth. She lowered her lids. But she knew the truth would scare him away.

"And what if I say it isn't enough? What then?"

For the first time she sensed an underlying tension within him. He frowned and stroked her cheek, tenderly. "I've always been honest with you. Told you what I want."

"You have."

"I'm just afraid that you'll want something I can't give. I'm not the man to build a future with, Emily. And if you want that, then you will be disappointed."

She swallowed hard, willing the sadness that flickered under the surface to descend further, somewhere where he, or she, could never see it.

She leaned towards him and broke the tension with a deep, passionate kiss.

"I'd be mad to want more than this." Her voice didn't sound like her own. Husky, like that of a woman who also lived for the present. Perhaps she could be that other woman. Perhaps she'd always been her.

But he didn't smile, merely put his arm around her and guided her back to the footpath. "Good."

THEY STROLLED up the Rue St Antoine in silence, both lost in their own thoughts. Hers were filled with confusion. One minute she felt like she belonged with Alessandro. She could do it: she could live the life, could feel the things he wanted her to feel. The next? Reality checks. She'd never lied to herself before. And wanting, simply wanting to be that other woman who lived in the present, wasn't enough.

He stopped outside a renaissance style, early seventeenth-century building. Uniformed staff allowed them entry into a courtyard. From there they walked into a further inner courtyard that lay at the heart of the beautiful building. Emily had never seen anything like it before in her life. The baroque-style architecture was designed to look like a theatre. At the centre of the theatre, musicians played, while all around people mingled. It was lit by thousands of candles, hooked up in sconces around the walls, high up to the third story, and by dozens of huge black wrought-iron standard candelabra. It was surreal.

"Some hotel this," she whispered to Alessandro while she ran her hand around the bas reliefs that decorated the walls.

He dropped his head to hers. "It's a private residence, Emily."

"Oh!" She could feel the heat of embarrassment flooding her face. If this was a private home, it wasn't like any she'd been in before. But, then, that was the difference between them, wasn't it?

"Darling Alex!"

Emily smelled the tall blonde's expensive perfume before

she heard her. "How has it been slumming it in Naples, darling, mixing with all those tradespeople?"

"Carisma, I'd like you to meet Emily."

Carisma turned to her for the first time. "Emily," she said uncertainly. "Welcome."

If only the tone of her voice and her body language echoed the sentiment, Emily reckoned she might have felt welcome.

"Hello. I'm one of those tradespeople."

Carisma's polite smile, widened stiffly before she turned once more to Alessandro. "So glad you came, darling. Come back to us as soon as you can. You must be missing your crowd." She glanced briefly towards Emily as if she were some strange memento from a parallel universe and walked away.

"Nice friends," Emily said curtly.

"Give them a chance, Emily. Carisma's led a sheltered life. You have to make allowances."

"Why should I make allowances for someone who's had a privileged life?"

"You don't, of course. Not, unless, that is, you want to get on with her. Which might be nice, don't you think."

It wasn't a question. It was a directive and Emily could feel her heels digging in, particularly easy as she had her highest heels on that night: black, patent with very, very thin spikes.

They walked further into the courtyard, Alessandro greeting people here and there. Emily took a glass from the waiter, along with a handful of nibbles while a group of beautiful people clustered around Alessandro.

"Alex!"

Alessandro introduced them, leaving the most beautiful until last.

"And this, Emily, is Ursula."

Ursula smiled with a warmth that made Emily forget, for just a moment, that she was an outsider.

As the others dominated Alessandro in conversation, Ursula drew Emily aside. She was a tall, statuesque, Swedish blonde.

"So, you're the reason for his disappearance," she said in a disarmingly accented English.

"Me? No. His work, his father…" Emily blustered and felt even more embarrassed when Ursula laughed.

"No. I think you are. You're different to his usual sort."

"That's not exactly a news flash, you know."

Ursula laughed. "Interesting, very interesting. I hope he sees what he has with you. I think he must."

"What makes you say that?"

"Because he usually comes alone to Paris."

"Really?"

"It is one of the rare times that we are able to meet. Our schedules are busy."

"Oh!" How could she have been so dumb? Ursula and Alessandro. Obviously. They were two beautiful people who no doubt had some kind of beautiful thing going on.

Ursula laughed. "Don't worry. It's not like that. I'd hoped it would be once. But now, it's just friendship. A close friendship."

Emily was trying to figure out how to establish exactly how close their friendship was when Ursula abruptly changed the subject.

"Now, tell me Emily, has Alessandro yet told you all about himself and about—"

Whatever Ursula was going to say was lost under the smothering bonhomie of a large group of people who had just arrived. They seemed to swallow Ursula whole and whisk her away with Ursula only able to wave. "Good luck, Emily, you're going to need it."

Emily was left alone, watching Ursula disappear. If Alessandro couldn't even commit to someone like Ursula, what hope did she have?

She turned to rejoin Alessandro but he'd moved away and was talking to a small group of people. If they'd all turned and smiled at that moment it would have looked like a photo from a society page in a fashion magazine. Emily sighed, sipped her wine and leaned against the pillar feeling defeated. He looked in his element: smiling, joking, totally engaged in that moment with his friends.

So different, so obviously different. The clothes didn't make her fit in. Nothing would make her fit in. She wasn't meant for him. She'd known it all along.

She looked up suddenly and saw him watching her. "Emily!" he beckoned for her to come. She could see that he couldn't easily move, trapped by the crowd of people.

She smiled and waved him off. "I'm going to find something to eat."

She didn't look back. He didn't need her.

The smell of food decided her route. In her discomfort, she'd downed several glasses of champagne in quick succession but it was food she wanted now.

"Looking for someone?" A tall, picture-perfect Englishman stood before her.

"No. Some*thing*. Food to be exact."

He laughed. "Allow me to show you." He cocked his head to one side and extended an arm. It was the best offer she'd had all night.

They filled up their plates and he took her to a secluded table.

"So, what brings you here, all alone."

"I'm not alone. My, er," for the life of her she didn't know how to describe her relationship with Alessandro. "My *friend* is circulating."

"Some friend," he leaned in to her.

"Yes, he is." She replied staunchly.

He shook his head.

She narrowed her eyes. "What's with the shaking of the head?"

"Come, Emily. No friend would leave you alone in a place you didn't know anyone."

"I told him to go. I was hungry and—"

"And he let you go."

She looked down at her food and ate with exaggerated concentration. "We're not here for long and he hasn't seen his friends in a while."

"So he leaves his girlfriend alone? That doesn't sound right to me."

"How exactly?"

"Perhaps you don't fit in here? You're English?"

"Well spotted."

"And not upper class. I can tell by your accent."

"And you are. I can tell by yours. So what?"

"Indeed. To us, 'so what'. But the others?" He shrugged. "There are snobs in this world, Emily." He'd shifted closer to her now. "People who don't appreciate what people like you have to offer. Now me, I appreciate everything you have to offer."

Despite Emily's new glasses, her gaze had grown blurry with the champagne. She pressed her eyes closed for a second and then opened them again to clear them. Nope, still the same. She turned away to try and focus her vision but when she turned the man appeared to be sitting closer to her and she could feel his breath down her cleavage.

She put her hand over her body, disliking the feel of his warm breath against her skin, and his eyes, devouring her. The intimacy was sudden and repulsive.

"Believe me. I have nothing to offer."

He smiled. "I don't. Believe you, that is."

"No really. You haven't a clue. It's true I don't belong here and it's just as true that I have nothing to offer."

"Just because your boyfriend doesn't value you, doesn't mean you should put yourself down."

Emily recoiled as his hand caressed her leg.

"No," she was suddenly startled.

"Come on. You're alone. Your boyfriend has found better things to do."

"That's not true."

"Come on, it doesn't sound like—"

"What, exactly, doesn't it sound like, Anthony?" Alessandro's words were icy with chill and menace.

Emily and Anthony both looked up, startled.

"Alex!" Anthony looked from Emily to Alessandro and his eyes widened with surprise. "*You* are Emily's 'friend'?"

"No, Anthony, I'm her lover. And I think it's time you went, don't you?"

Emily closed her eyes and rubbed her throbbing head. When she opened them there was no sign of Anthony.

"Everything all right, Emily?"

She sighed and leaned back against the leather couch. "Of course. Fine. And you? Did you enjoy catching up with your friends?"

He took her hand. "To start with, yes. But I wanted to be with you. I was also concerned that you might be lonely."

She smiled. The smile turned into a laugh and part of her heard it and thought it inappropriate. The other part didn't care any more.

"I'm used to being alone, *Alex*," she laid emphasis on his name, hating the Anglicization of it. All his friends called him that. It seemed a denial of his nationality, of who he was.

He looked away. She could feel him distancing himself from her. So the process had begun already. The test was complete. She didn't fit into his world and she would have to leave.

"I'm sorry. I thought you would enjoy the party."

She shrugged lightly. "The food's good."

"I was wrong."

She dropped her fork onto the plate with a clatter and pushed the plate away.

"Hey. I'm sorry. I just don't fit in. Despite the clothes, despite the money spent on them, I just don't fit in. What's that wonderful expression?" She squeezed her eyes in concentration. "You can't make a silk purse from a sow's ear."

Alessandro slammed down his drink so hard that the glass shattered and white wine slid across the table amidst shards of glass. He grabbed her hand, his dark sleeve studded with glass, and darkening even further as it soaked up the wine.

"What, Emily, do I have to do to make you believe in yourself? Hey?"

"Well, perhaps, spending time with me instead of wandering off with your friends, might be a start."

"I thought you were talking with Ursula. She's a good lady. I thought you were OK."

"She's fine. But then she left." Her short, perfunctory laugh told all. "Story of my life. But back to you. You're in your element here, not me. I'm sorry. I thought, for just one second, that I might be. But I'm not." She flicked a look at her watch. "I need to go, with or without you."

She held his gaze for long seconds while neither spoke.

"Without me? Emily, it's not exactly a taxi ride back to Naples."

"Then with you. Whatever. It makes no difference. I want to keep to the terms of your father's will, even if you don't. I won't lose this position."

"Emily. My father's stipulation was for you to have the

position. Only you. You cannot lose it. It's always been yours."

She didn't feel herself recoil but, minutes later, wondered how she'd managed to move so far away from him.

"You, you made me think that I had to do as you say, otherwise I'd lose the job. You devious bastard." Her voice was soft with restrained anger.

"I was not lying. You had to stay there. It's just that I didn't tell you that it was your name that my father stipulated. I also had to stay there. He'd always envisaged just the two of us."

"What did he want from me? Some kind of amusement for his son?"

"I think he had you more in mind as some kind of savior."

She stood up and stumbled out of the mansion, unaware of the looks of people, unaware of her surroundings. It was only when she was walking back that she felt his arm come around her, and keep her from falling.

"I'm sorry, Emily. You must believe that I feel deeply for you. You must believe that."

She shook her head in confusion. "I don't know what to believe any more. I just need to get back."

He stopped her and held her tight.

"You're not going anywhere until you hear me out. Emily, me and you, right now, have nothing to do with my father. I want you here. I need you here."

She shook her head. "I don't belong."

"Of course you do. I don't care about the rest of them but you belong with me."

He lifted her chin and she saw that his face was streaked with yellow light in the Parisian gloom. He dipped his face to hers and caught her lips in a kiss that was designed to be gentle. But she wasn't feeling gentle. Her body's needs were paramount and she expressed it all in that kiss.

It was Alessandro who pulled away, his breath coming fast. She pushed herself against him, taking satisfaction in his arousal.

"No, Emily, wait." Alessandro's voice was dominant and strong. He pushed her away and turned on his cell phone. "I'm taking you to the plane straight away."

SHE LAY on the bed of the aircraft in the darkness that she had insisted upon, sated and relaxed. Making love with Alessandro was all she now craved. But, unlike anything else she knew, unlike any food she knew, once she'd tasted it, it simply stimulated her appetite for more. And more.

Then why was she crying? She wiped her face with the back of her hand—first one cheek and then another—and gently dropped her hand back to her side. Alessandro lay unmoving beside her. She didn't think he was asleep—his breathing wasn't relaxed enough—but he, like her, was obviously in no mood for talking.

It was dark now. But daylight would come soon. Today had shown her that it didn't matter how she looked, she would never fit into his life. He didn't understand. But he would. How long did she have before he discovered her secrets and left her? It was just a matter of time. Sooner or later he'd discover she wasn't the perfect woman, that she wasn't for him. She could sit around and wait or she could act.

And waiting was one thing Emily was never very good at.

CHAPTER 7

*E*mily's cell phone vibrated in her pocket and the sound of fire crackers—a ring-tone courtesy of a university bonfire night celebration—filled the air.

"Em! Phone's going again."

She dug it out of the pocket of her baggy shorts, checked the number and killed it, slipped it back in her pocket and carried on making notes on that day's dig.

Emily's team looked up in surprise then exchanged puzzled glances. Emily could feel their surprise from beneath her lowered lids.

"Don't sweat it. I'm busy, that's all."

Let them think what they liked. It was out of character because she always answered her cell phone, not least because it rang so rarely. It was usually about work and that was all that mattered to her.

But the calls she'd been receiving all day had nothing to do with work.

Just the memory of Alessandro made her body flush with heat.

Closely followed by anger that she'd let herself be

seduced quite so thoroughly: had left herself open to hurt, quite so stupidly.

She rubbed her shoulder. One of the deeper scars was aching today. It always did when there was damp in the air. The knife had gone deeper there—had snagged at her nerve endings. She had no sensation, other than an ache in the cold and damp.

She looked into the late afternoon sky. The sun was dulled by a thin film of cloud. She'd been right. A storm was coming. The hills that surrounded the estate were grey in the dimming light.

She scuffed some of the stones underfoot, her mind miles away from her work, for once.

He needed to know. He needed to see her for what she was: a freak—only good for telling the weather.

"Em to earth—come in!"

Emily turned to find Sue in front of her, hands on hips, irritation on her face.

"What's up?"

"You. That's what. I don't know what the hell's got into you today. You've been mooching around—"

"Hey, I don't mooch."

"Mooching around like some lovelorn teenager. If I didn't know you better I'd say you'd got man problems."

Emily glared at Sue. "I'm not even going to dignify that with a reply."

"Ah, so you have got man problems."

Emily continued to write.

"Hey, Em!"

"I'm ignoring you, in case you haven't noticed."

"Ignore me all you like but I've been trying to tell you that you've some corporate guy standing over there politely calling your name while you've been staring into the hills. What's got into you?"

A discreet cough behind her made her turn around, belatedly following her team's stares.

One of Alessandro's assistants stood behind her. He looked her up and down. "Signorina? Are you ready?"

"For what?"

"The conte has asked me to take you to the Rovella townhouse for the supper. He apologizes for not coming himself, but he's tied up with meetings until later."

"I know nothing of the supper."

"If you'd answered your cell, Em, you just might."

Emily glowered at her friend.

"The conte asked me to tell you that there would be important benefactors for you to meet tonight, including trustees of the Museo Archeologico Nazionale."

Emily scowled again. She couldn't refuse that and he knew it.

She passed the clipboard and notes to her friend. "Here. You take over."

"Have a lovely time Em." She grinned at Emily. "If you need anything just sing out."

Emily didn't reply but gave her friend a black look. Sue knew Emily hated such occasions. What she didn't know was that, for the first time, she wouldn't have to borrow Sue's clothes. She had enough of her own now.

But half an hour later, showered and dressed, Emily's hand skimmed over the beautiful clothes Alessandro had bought for her and plucked the same red dress she'd worn the first night she'd met him. She still hadn't given it back to Sue. For some reason she'd kept it hanging with the other utilitarian items in her wardrobe. She ran her hand down its length now, remembering that night.

But memories weren't the reason she'd chosen it tonight. The clothes Alessandro had bought her were beautiful and more suitable, but lacking in one particular——they all covered her scarred shoulders and back.

And tonight she had a point to make.

ALESSANDRO LISTENED GRIMLY to the group of businessmen who'd been invited to the party and pulled his tie loose from the knot.

He took the last swig of his whisky and held up his glass for the waiter to refill it.

Why the hell hadn't she answered his phone calls?

What had been so important that she'd left their bed before the sun had risen?

Their lovemaking had changed from a wild, sensual experience to something more intense, if anything.

Why had she regretted it then?

He wasn't used to anyone—least of all a woman—not returning his calls. The last time that had happened his wife had left him, taking their son with her. The last time that had happened he'd lost his temper—seen red—and got into a fight with his wife's lover that had resulted in his son's death.

The bile that the memory brought to his mouth made him angry, a potent reminder of the melee of feelings he still kept hidden, locked, deep inside. If she regretted her actions, then so did he. He flicked a look at his watch, oblivious to the woman talking to him until her curious gaze, as she looked down at the poolside, drew his attention.

"Oh my God! What on earth happened to her?"

From their vantage point on the mezzanine floor above the pool, he could see down Emily's generous cleavage but it wasn't that which had caused the woman's remark.

Emily's hair was piled high and her shoulders were completely bare: no covering scarf, no jacket, nothing but a tracery of white scars, highlighted against her tanned skin.

The wounds were vicious: some wide, some jagged, some puckered, but all discolored in the evening light, yellowed by the oncoming storm.

At that moment she'd stopped her slow progress along the poolside and looked up. Their eyes met: hers fiery and angry, full of a defensive fury that he didn't understand.

She took a sip from her glass of wine and then turned away.

Alessandro beckoned to one of his assistants.

Within minutes he'd returned with Emily in tow.

She walked up to him, her defensive anger almost palpable.

"I've been summoned, it would seem."

Alessandro gritted his teeth in an effort to control his anger.

"Emily, allow me to introduce the patrons of the Museo Archeologico Nazionale."

He slipped his arm around her, his hands gently relaxed on her scarred shoulders.

"Gentleman, this is Emily Carlyle, my close friend and archaelogist for the estate."

Alessandro barely heard them exchange pleasantries. He had eyes only for Emily. If she was angry, he was now more so, except he was better at hiding it.

"Emily, the gentlemen would like to hear about your finds at the estate. Perhaps you could enlighten them?"

He could hear the chill in his voice and he could see that she registered it.

"Of course."

She turned her back slightly on Alessandro, allowing him to see the full extent of her injuries. It angered him even further. How could anyone do such a thing?

Then the face of his wife's lover slammed into his mind— bloody and terrified. His wife and her lover had threatened to take his child away with them and blind anger had seized him when he had taken hold of the lover. He couldn't remember being stopped. He could only remember the blood.

His hand fell from her shoulders.

SHE'D NEVER SEEN him so cold or so angry before. Not that she knew him well, she reminded herself. But she'd trusted him implicitly, guided by his actions, his touch, his words. She'd trusted her own instincts. But seeing his rage simmering beneath that cool façade, had she been wrong?

She gave the minimum of information of the dig to the patrons. She was suspicious of their interest, of this meeting, and now of Alessandro's motives.

As soon as she'd finished Alessandro excused themselves, took her firmly by the hand and pulled her across the room, towards his personal suite.

She yanked her hand back but he continued to hold it. People milled around them, interested glances shot their way, but the drinks and music and laughter continued to surge like waves around them.

"I think there's little point in going anywhere more private."

"Fine. Just tell me what the hell you think you're doing?"

So he was embarrassed after all. It had all been a show.

"I don't see what gives you the right to be so damned angry. It wasn't you that was stared at and whispered about as you walked through the room." She jutted her chin up in defiance. "You didn't have to acknowledge me as your 'close friend'."

His eyes flared with intense exasperation and anger and he looked away briefly. When he turned to her again his face was grim with self control. "You're trying to prove some sort of point?"

"I thought it time to show you what I'm really like. I'm not perfect."

"Really?" Sarcasm dripped from the word. He held her stare before her gaze dropped in defeat. "Tell me *cara*, who is?"

He turned and looked around the room angrily as if trying to restrain his temper.

"You for one."

"Don't be ridiculous. For all your intelligence you're acting like a child."

"If it's childish to show you what I'm really like, then I guess I am."

"And what are you like?"

"I'm not for you." Her voice had dropped to a whisper, the mixed emotions refusing to give it power.

"I think that's up to me to decide. We are lovers—"

She pulled her head up sharply, interrupting him. "And you regret it, of course."

He tugged at her hand, his anger barely restrained. "How could I regret feeling you orgasm as you slowly slipped over me for the first time? How can I regret the intensity in your eyes when you look at me, silently, when our bodies blend together as one?"

Heat flushed through her, her mouth went dry as she felt her insides clench and moisten at the memory. She looked around, suddenly aware of conversations being hushed nearby as people strained to hear.

"OK, let's go somewhere more quiet."

"No. You chose this. See it out." His grip on her arm tightened. "How could I regret holding your body, tasting your breasts? I want you now."

"Alessandro. You're hurting me."

It was as if he'd been slapped and the anger left his face. He dropped her arm. "I'm sorry."

"I shouldn't have come."

"I invited you. There were people I wanted you to see. Work I wanted you to do."

"That's it. Work?"

"And, I wanted to see you again—somewhere more social, somewhere other than the estate. It seems this was a mistake. It seems that it's you who regret our relationship. Strange. I didn't seem so repugnant to you when we lay naked together."

She shook her head. "What are you talking about?"

"It seems that you think this little performance will turn me off you. There can be only one reason for that. As I say you obviously regret it."

She shook her head, unable to contradict him, unable to tell the truth.

"I've come to show you what I really am. I couldn't last night. But I have no place in your life—short or long term— and I wanted to show you why."

"Why?"

She grabbed hold of his hand and forced him to touch her shoulder.

"*I*, am damaged goods. I thought that much is clear."

"*You*, need your head examining, in that much you are correct. If you think a few scars would upset me, then you have no idea who I am or anything about me."

"You are rich, aristocratic and beautiful. I am none of these things."

"So, I should have nothing to do with you then?"

"Why would you want to?"

He pulled her tight against her and she could feel his arousal. "I want you now, as much as I did last night, more even. It's you that yearns for a superficial perfection, not me.

I want a real body." He ran his hands over her hips and held them there.

She looked around, suddenly embarrassed.

"Move your hands, people are looking."

He pulled her round a corner, out of sight of the others. "Like this?" He moved one hand down and caressed her bottom, curving round and then under before resting there.

She pushed away his hands but he was angry now.

"You think me so shallow, Emily. It is you who's the snob with your pre-conceived notions about what I should and shouldn't want. You have no idea. No thought for anything other than yourself."

"I—"

But her words were cut off by a kiss, more savage than he'd ever given her. Heat and power seared her mouth. She couldn't help responding, her whole body wanted him. Too soon his lips pulled away, his forehead leaning against hers. Their panting breaths mingled for long seconds before he retook her hand, pulled away and stepped towards the nearest door, pulling her after him.

Blindly she followed, down a long corridor, stumbling after him, nothing real except for the urgent needs of their bodies. It was only when the door slammed behind them that she realized they'd entered his private suite.

She fell back against the door, his body pressed tight against her so that she could feel every taut muscle, every part of his hard body, straining, needing her. It gave her a sense of power she exulted in as she met his tongue with her own with an urgency felt in every part of her body. Desperate to feel his skin against hers, she pushed her hands under his shirt and skimmed his bunched muscles before descending and slipping her hands beneath his trousers. She could feel the effect of her hands as he groaned into her mouth.

He pulled away from her then and, with one swift movement, pulled down the strapless dress so that it lay in folds around her waist, her breasts spilling out over the soft cloth and into his waiting hands. With his thumb and forefinger he rubbed her nipples until she was aching with need; with his tongue he invaded her open mouth and with his leg he shifted his weight between hers, urging her to open them.

She didn't need any urging. She needed him quite as much as he wanted her and with a flick of a button and a careful easing of a zip, she found what she wanted.

With a frustrated grunt he pulled up her dress, until it lay in one ruched layer around her stomach and pulled down her panties. Impatiently she pulled down his trousers and he picked her up in one swift movement.

Wrapping her legs around his body, she arched her back to try to get close to him. Hampered by his trousers, he cursed and stamped out of them. With one swift thrust he pinned against the wall. For one long, ecstatic moment she thought she would faint from the exquisite sensations that coursed through her body. She came with his second thrust. The door rattled with each penetration, banging against the door jamb, as relentless as it was rhythmic. There was no accommodation for her orgasm, no waiting, no caresses, no time for seduction this time. Only the sound of the thudding of the door gaining in momentum, stirring her body once more until the coils of sensation joined in with his rhythm and she cried out as they climaxed in unison: his seed pumping deep within her.

She slumped against him then, spent. Her head rested on his shoulder as they both waited for their frenetic breathing to subside and for reality to slowly re-assert itself. Everything had been in that moment, within themselves; there had been no room in their consciousness for anything external. But slowly, the ticking of a clock, the far-off laughter and shouts of the party-goers and the buzzing of a fly as it angrily battered itself, time after time, at the window, slowly these sounds penetrated both of them, bringing them back to reality.

His grip on her thighs relaxed and allowed her legs to slide in his grasp until she stood trembling before him. Still they had not looked each other in the eye. Her forehead was buried in his chest, lost between his warm skin and his disheveled shirt whose buttons lay on the floor where he or she—she didn't know who—must have ripped it open. It was only when she pulled away that she noticed the smears of mascara on his white shirt. Shakily, she wiped her eyes with her fingers.

"You're crying." His fingers traced the same arc as hers had just wiped.

She shook her head.

"I'm so sorry, Emily."

Then she looked up in to his eyes but he avoided her gaze and looked away. As if to emphasize the distance that was falling between them, he released his grip and his hands, slowly, very slowly dropped to his sides.

"Alessandro?"

Her eyes still seeking his, she wriggled back into her dress, covering her confusion as to the sudden distance by concentrating on covering her nakedness.

"Alessandro?" Her voice was stronger now. He had to be made to see.

He pulled up her top more securely, his hands hesitated on her shoulders.

"I'm sorry."

He looked at her then and she wished he hadn't. His eyes were bleak with despair. She shook her head. All her previous anger had disappeared. "No."

"I shouldn't have done that."

"No. You're wrong. It wasn't just you. I wanted it."

But he'd walked away, across to the window where the sickly light of the setting sun now entered the room.

"You wanted it? I don't think you know what you want. Do you?"

She made a step towards him and then stopped because she didn't know how to reply.

She could feel the tears now as they tracked down her face.

"I wanted you then. Before? I still wanted you but I needed to show you that I'm not meant for you. Not meant for your world."

"And you think you're the better judge of that than me."

She nodded hesitantly.

"And you'd go to such public lengths to save me from myself."

She nodded again.

"Perhaps you're right, Emily. If you suppose me to be so shallow, so superficial, then perhaps we shouldn't be together."

Her heart was breaking as he tenderly traced the line of her face, her cheekbone and her jaw before stopping at the neck.

"But, Emily, what you don't understand is that I knew. I knew from the first evening we met. I saw your scars and they meant nothing to me except that I wanted to make sure you never felt such pain again."

She shook her head. The tears now unstoppable.

"I didn't know. I thought you'd be disgusted."

He closed his eyes. "You have a very low opinion of me." He walked away and crossed his arms. "But the worst of it is, that you're right. You bring out the worst in me. I've never taken a woman with so little finesse, against the wall. Dio!" He looked around disgusted. "I don't behave like that." He spoke between gritted teeth. "I lose control when I'm with you. You break it down."

She tried to touch his shoulder. "Alessandro." He shook her hand off. "Listen to me. I wanted you as much as you wanted me. Come," she tried to encircle his body with her arms, "let's make love again. Properly this time." She reached up to kiss him but his eyes remained open, cool.

"Emily." He reached up to her hands but instead of a caress, he pulled them back down to their sides. "I can't risk it. Losing control again."

She shook her head. "I don't understand."

"It's the past."

"Ha! You and your stupid phobia about the past. Tell me. Tell me!"

"I lost control in a fight once. I nearly killed a man."

"You what?"

"Lucky for him, and for me, that a friend pulled me off him in time."

"So, it was a one-off. He survived. You learned from it."

"No. It was more than that. My anger and stupidity led to the death of someone dear to me."

"Oh," her voice was soft. He'd loved and lost. No wonder he had no interest in the future. He'd had all he wanted in the past and blamed himself for its loss. He couldn't look back and he couldn't look forward. Doomed to remain in the present, the place of everlasting forgetfulness. "And I make you remember?"

He nodded. "You make me remember everything that I want to forget—everything about me, about what I'm capable of, that I want to forget."

In vain, Emily tried to quell the rising panic. "So, what are you saying? That it's over?"

"I don't know. Just that perhaps you were right that we weren't meant to be together. Except for different reasons."

She stepped away from him. She'd succeeded and yet she felt defeated. She didn't want to push him away now. She wanted him close, with her, forever.

"But I was wrong. I'm so sorry. My scars have been with me for so many years—affecting everything that they seemed bigger than everything, even you. They skew my thinking, my feelings, always."

He shook his head. "I understand. But perhaps if your feelings were true, then they wouldn't. Perhaps if your feelings for me were stronger, then a few scars wouldn't have been able to come between us. But my darling Emily, your scars are visible and easier to deal with. It is mine that you've uncovered now. And they're impossible to deal with. I'm sorry."

His eyes were chill; his jaw was set in a hard line where the muscles clenched with control.

"It's too late, isn't it?" Her voice sounded as distant as the look in his eyes.

He nodded. "It's too late."

He watched her go and wanted her to stop. But he closed his eyes instead, willing himself not to call out after her. And as his eyes closed he remembered the last time he'd felt this angry. He remembered not wanting to stop as he hit his wife's lover and he remembered the fear on the face of Niccy, his son, just before his wife had taken him and driven off, into a tree, killing them both outright.

No. He was right. Losing control like that with Emily was a vivid reminder of his weakness and the damage it could wreak. He could never again afford to lose control. Particularly with Emily. He had to protect her from himself because as much as he tried to repress any violent tendencies by repressing all emotions altogether, Emily seemed to be a key that unlocked and unleashed things that he'd thought were long dead.

He looked around as if awoken from a stupor, noted the pale light, weak and threatening, and the sounds of his party continuing, oblivious to the scene just acted out. Laughter, talking, music. He needed a drink.

With sudden decision he strode back into the party and began talking to a slender blonde, sleekly dressed in the latest fashion, not a hair out of place. She'd do. He didn't even notice her face, her looks, her conversation. He sought only oblivion.

HE DIDN'T EVEN NOTICE when Emily turned, retraced her steps and watched as he flirted outrageously—and effectively —with the tall blonde. He didn't notice her turn, almost stumble into a waiter, before running out of the room.

CHAPTER 8

*T*he leather chair squeaked as Alessandro pushed it back and put his feet on the table, swinging the chair to an angle so that he could tap the pen on the desk, turn it once, tap again and turn again.

The tapping sound somehow helped to keep him tethered to the here and now: its repetitive staccato, an appeal from his mind to his emotions to stay on track. But they kept swerving off-course with glimpses of his son like half-forgotten, faded snapshots, flicking randomly through his brain.

His son's hands, plump and softly rounded with stubby, unformed fingers topped by half-bitten nails. The memory of those ragged nails spiked his heart—a reminder of his son's timid nature which he'd been unable to reassure.

He tapped the pen more loudly on the glass-topped desk, keeping in time with the second hand of an antique clock, once a possession of his father's.

Again his son's face, that last night, white with shock. Alessandro hadn't known that he was there. It had only been when Alessandro's friend had pulled him off Eva's lover, when the pounding anger lessened that he'd turned and seen his son's stricken face watching him. It had been only a few seconds during which Eva had hurled abuse at him and, when Alessandro had approached, wanting to get close to his son, to explain, to reassure that he wasn't the monster the boy had just seen, Eva had grabbed his son and half-dragged him to the car.

He'd seen that the boy's seat belt wasn't fastened. He'd seen it and he'd been unable to do a thing about it when Eva had hurled the car around the drive, skidding before she'd accelerated down the long icy drive from which they were never to emerge alive.

Alessandro stabbed the desk with the point of his steel-tipped pen; the metallic sound echoing around the hard-surfaced interior. But it made no difference. He rubbed his eyes and looked bleakly out of the window. His focus on the present was weakening.

He'd not felt the vividness of the pain for years. He'd buried the acute agony of the knowledge that, despite his love for his son, he'd failed him. He'd caused his death. He'd buried it deep. And he'd turned away from the memories, unable to endure them.

And then Emily had come along.

She'd broken down that barrier between him and his past by making him feel again.

The face of his son morphed into Emily's green eyes. They drew him in until he forgot himself in their verdant secrets.

She was a key to the past he could not forget and which he couldn't bear to remember. She touched him like the vibration of a note on a stringed instrument, bypassing all his thought processes, finding its home at his core. He could no more control the effect of her than stop breathing.

And what had he done with this woman who'd worked

magic over his emotions? He'd taken her without finesse, without protection. He'd damaged her as surely as he had his son; as surely as the perpetrator of her scars had done. He could not be trusted with love. He couldn't be trusted.

"Cazzo!" He flung the pen down the table until it skittered to a halt by a model of a building.

Someone coughed and removed the offending pen.

He looked up, surprised to see four pairs of eyes looking at him as if he'd lost the plot.

He shrugged. "Cosa?" Perhaps he had lost the plot because his story was turning out to be a pretty twisted affair.

"Cosa?" He asked more loudly this time, demanding a response, turning from one to the other. But none was forthcoming. Suddenly he felt very tired. He gestured to the miniature complex of buildings. "Proceed."

He swung the chair so that he had his back to the table and stood up and walked to the window.

The sky was black and the rain had begun to pour. The storm was nearly upon them. They happened infrequently in Campania but when they did they could be brutal.

They could destroy everything in their path.

He turned to look at his staff discussing the removal of slum dwellings on the development site.

He closed his eyes and pinched his nose. He was sick of destruction.

The rain pounded against the window, the premature evening closing in upon him, intensifying his need to escape his ghosts. But the prime offender now stared back at him: his reflection looked demonic in the darkened glass.

He could get away. Go, as far away from her as possible. The storm provided the perfect excuse. If it was as bad as they forecast the precarious road to the estate could become blocked. At least it would give him an excuse to stay in the city. The solicitor couldn't hold that against him. It would be a relief not to lie so close to her at the villa and not have her in his arms: not be haunted by his past, by his feelings. Wouldn't it?

He groaned and closed his eyes.

But it was too late for that.

It had been too late from the minute he'd laid eyes on her: the body with which he needed to connect and the mind and spirit that moved and played and sang in tune with his own.

He ground his fist into his other fist, summoning up the aggression that he needed to resist her.

"Conte?"

When he turned to the meeting, he realized that they must have been calling him for some time, that they'd moved on to the development of the villa estate.

"Si?"

"The plans are going well. The concept is one of contrasts. The Aphrodite Mosaic will be encased in Perspex and a centerpiece to the foyer of the spa. The designers see a monochrome color scheme—white with steel—sharp angles and clean lines.

"And the ruins?"

"As the ultimate back-drop—a talking point."

Alessandro shook his head and his fingers worried the amber piece of tessera he kept in his pocket. The one Emily had shown him that first night. "A talking point."

"As you, yourself, suggested at our previous meeting," replied the perplexed-looking executive.

"Right. No, you are correct. It is exactly as we planned."

Then why had the world shifted and the plans suddenly not look so brilliant any more?

"We were also saying that the planning for the new development is at a crucial stage now. Any more archaeological excavation could be counter-productive. We can use what we've discovered so far but any more and the state will intervene."

"Si." He nodded wearily. He knew all about the regulations. And he knew that the day he had to tell Emily that she could no longer dig at the estate, would signal the absolute end to their relationship.

But not yet. Now there was time. What the hell was he waiting for?

He turned and looked at the grey rain lashing the building. The bay had disappeared—the water and sky had become one. He hoped he hadn't left it too late.

THE LIGHTNING LIT up the dull afternoon and the thunder echoed so loudly around the dig that some of the team shrieked and clapped their hands over their ears.

"Let's call it a day, Em. We can't see anyway." Sue looked around the dig anxiously. "Let's get some tarpaulins over this section. It looks like there might be some flooding."

"Get the tarps in place but let's keep going while there's light. And when the light goes we have torches. Time's running out. And, if we get the go-ahead to extend the excavation, which we should do, we'll have a heap more work to do."

Even Emily's enthusiasm couldn't blind her to the increasing chill and heaviness of the rain that soaked them to the skin within minutes.

But it was the atmosphere that got to her. The light was strangely yellow as the storm built. Anaemic, jaundiced, sick.

She felt a shiver run down her back.

"OK," she shouted to the others. "Let's get inside."

They raced through the dissolving ground back up through the overgrown gardens to the villa.

They tumbled inside laughing and shaking themselves.

She pulled the doors closed with effort against the wind.

"Man, where did that come from?" Sue asked.

"It's been brewing for some time. You could feel it in the air." Emily gazed out at the wind and the others exchanged glances. "And it's meant to get worse."

"At least there's no electricity to go off," Sue giggled nervously.

"What?" Emily looked around as if suddenly aware of her surroundings. "I'll turn on the gas lamps. It's like night in here."

"If it's going to get worse, we'd best get back to the cottages." One of the young students looked anxiously at the sky.

"And leave Em here, alone?"

"I'll be all right. You guys go. You're right. Go to the cottages and we'll get back to work as soon as the rain stops."

"You sure?" The young student was already dragging at Sue's hand.

"Sure I'm sure. There's enough security roaming the estate. I'll be fine."

"And there's the count," Sue raised her an eyebrow. "He'll keep you company."

"Perhaps, perhaps not. Anyway, you go. I've paperwork to do."

"I'm glad the count will be here. This place is too damn creepy, with or without guards."

Emily watched her team run outside, shrieking loudly as the cold rain slapped their wet bodies once more.

EMILY CHANGED, twisted her long hair into a towel and made herself a coffee. She wandered back to the office from the kitchen, checking on the rooms, feeling vaguely uneasy. It was stupid. She was just off-balance at the moment, more susceptible to others' fears.

She towel-dried her hair and curled up in an armchair to do her paperwork. The reports that needed compiling for the university's sabbatical and research committees, the proposals for the dig in Antioch, updating budgets for the current dig etc, etc, etc. It was never-ending and the least favorite part of her job.

She didn't notice the daylight leach out of the room, little by little. Under the small pool of light the gas lamp emitted, Emily was oblivious to the fact that she was surrounded by utter darkness as she continued to work.

It was only when her stomach groaned that she realized dinner-time had been and gone. She looked at her watch. Then peered at it. It was gone ten. She glanced around and listened. No sign of Alessandro. No sign of any guards or staff. But then Alessandro had dismissed the guards from around the villa. She remembered now. He'd said he'd look after the villa.

She rose, stretched and peered out of the window. He should be here soon. It was still raining heavily. Raindrops drummed down onto the roof of the loggia, spilling over the gutters, thundering onto the terrazza below. She went outside onto the loggia, safe from the rain and smelled the wild night—the sodden earth, the fragrance from the crushed flowers. No lights. No guards. Nobody. She was entirely alone.

She swallowed the hint of fear that threatened to surface.

EMILY ATE a cursory meal of whatever she could find in the larder. No staff had turned up that night. It was the first time.

She wished she hadn't let the others leave quite so easily.

She shivered, locked up the villa and went to bed and lay listening to the wind battering the old building that creaked and groaned under the barrage.

Suddenly there was a crash and she looked out the window. Her heart was pounding, but it was just a terracotta roof tile that had fallen onto the terrazza.

She drew the shutters together once more and sat back on the bed.

God, she couldn't do this. She'd wander over to the cottages. If she got chucked off the job, so be it. But it wasn't as if anyone was around to notice.

She put on her wet weather gear and went out into the garden that was now like a lake surrounded by mud. Head down against the rain and wind, she trudged up the drive and checked the gates. They were open and there was no security to be seen. Stunned, Emily stumbled into the shadows, under the shelter of the huge trees that groaned and cracked in the fierce wind. No security, she repeated to herself as if trying to impress upon her numbed mind the severity of the situation. Even if there was no security for the house, they should still have been around the estate. Something must have gone wrong. She peered down the rough, metal road. It clung to the hillside and twisted sharply out of sight. It was possible that there had been a rock fall or mudslide that had effectively cut her off from Naples.

Still, her friends were on the other side of the estate.

And she wasn't afraid. Was she?

Tentatively she emerged out of the shelter of the trees and found the perimeter path to the cottages. But before she'd taken two steps she stopped and grimaced. She'd left her cell phone behind. If anyone needed her she wouldn't know. Not, she told herself sternly that she was expecting a call from Alessandro. After all he hadn't bothered to contact her all day.

His words still rang in her ears. It was obvious he'd meant them. She was as bad as all the others with her facile judgments, making assumptions about other people that were really her own.

Was he right? Was it she who was obsessed with perfection, not anyone else? Was *she* the superficial, shallow one?

Absorbed in her thoughts she returned to the house and ran up the stairs.

She grabbed her cell phone and checked it for the hundredth time that day. Then she froze. The wind had died down momentarily and she distinctly heard the back door bang shut in the wind.

She'd locked it before she'd left. Someone had managed to pick the lock and enter the villa.

A cold sweat swept over her.

Marcus. The vision of his face—round, bland and cruel—forced itself into her mind.

She shook her head. It couldn't be. She was haunted by phantoms.

Probably just one of the team had come to check to see if she was OK.

She forced herself to step towards the door. She thanked God she hadn't bothered to turn on the gas lights, knowing as she had where her cell phone would be.

Now, at least, she didn't advertise her presence.

At first she couldn't hear anything. That alone made her realize it couldn't be any of her team. Instead of relaxing she tensed, stayed out of sight, and listened.

One by one she identified the sounds, straining to hear anything above and beyond the strengthening storm.

Rain battered the villa and the wind in the trees tore and whistled through the branches. But above that she heard something else: sounds that numbed her mind with fear.

The creak of the wooden stairs as some kind of pressure

was exerted on their surface was followed by the soft thud of a second foot joining the first on the hollow step.

Feet shuffled on the landing as they went to move forward but instead, paused at the first bedroom before entering, moving and then leaving the room again.

Another step, closer now.

Her heart thudded wildly.

It had to be Marcus. Who else? The treasures weren't here were they? What else, *who* else, could the person be searching for, but her? He'd told her that he'd come back for her, that she hadn't seen the last of him. She knew them to be the ramblings of someone who was mentally ill but what if the treatment he'd received hadn't worked? What if he really had come back for her now, to finish off what he'd started?

She clenched her hand over the phone and an idea flashed into her mind.

As the steps approached she quickly and silently selected her ring-tone and, putting it on to the loudest setting, held it up to the open door.

The sound of her friends screaming and yelling as fireworks exploded around them filled the air, followed by the cracking sounds of two rockets launching and exploding. They sounded like gunshots in the empty, echoing hall. She picked up a trowel in the other hand, opened the door wide, shone the light of her torch down the hall and threw it with all her might. But whoever it was had his back to her and was half way down the stairs and would have been aware only of the thud of the metal trowel against the wooden handrail.

Emily collapsed against the wall as she heard the intruder run out of the villa.

She crawled over to the open window and strained to hear him leave the grounds.

She was rewarded with an abbreviated shout of laughter or perhaps it was just the shriek of the wind straining through the tangle of ancient branches in the thick canopy overhead?

Whatever. It struck chills through to her soul.

He'd be back. He thought he'd escaped a trap but he'd be back. She'd frightened him off for now. But if it was Marcus —and she felt a bone-deep chill certainty that it was—then he'd find another way to come for her.

She flicked opened her cell once more and tried to call Alessandro but there was no coverage. All she could do was to sit and wait for either Alessandro to come or Marcus. But the hours passed—slowly, stiffly, chillingly—and Alessandro didn't come.

No-one came.

ALESSANDRO SLAMMED on the brakes of the four-wheel drive in a shower of mud in the dark early hours of the morning. Despite his exhaustion, caused by working alongside the road crew to shift the mudslide that had blocked the road to the villa, he jumped out onto the sodden lawn and ran over to the villa.

He burst through the door and stopped in his tracks.

There, in the corner, cradling some vicious-looking archaeological tools, Emily was slumped, sound asleep.

He felt sickened to see this strong woman in such a vulnerable position. He should have been there. He cursed himself for their stupid argument that meant nothing now. Not beside this. Not beside Emily. She could have been hurt. She needed him and he hadn't been there for her.

He crouched down beside her.

"Emily." He stroked her arm. She moaned, rolled her head and blinked her eyes open. Her eyes slowly focused on him.

"You're here," she said sleepily and smiled.

The tension of the night had disappeared. "I'm here. Just a little late."

The trowels and knives clattered onto the tiles as she released them from her grip.

"What the—?" She jumped up. "Where were you? I've been here all night. Alone!"

He took her in his arms. "I know. I couldn't get to you. I'm so sorry, Emily. I let you down. No-one could get to you. The road was blocked. Are you OK?"

She began to pace across the room, back and forth. She stopped suddenly, raked her hair back off her face and turned to face him.

"He was here, Alessandro. He was here." Tears coursed down her face. "He was here," she said more softly, her face contorting with a pain that found a corresponding pain within him.

"I know." He drew her close to him and stroked her hair, desperate to give comfort, to extinguish the fear he could see in her eyes. "The security guards found him."

"You have him?" She pulled away, relief and disbelief filling her face in equal measure.

"He had no choice but to return by the main road. We caught him at the road block."

She slumped into his arms and sobbed. "I thought he'd got me again. I thought he would hurt me again. I thought—"

"What do you mean, 'again'? The man was a professional thief. He hurt you?"

"What?" She got up, shaking her head. "No. He's not a thief. He'd come up the stairs, looking for me."

"Looking for family treasures. That's where people keep their valuables. And he knew it."

"No. You've got it wrong. It was him."

"Tell me, Emily, what happened? Who was it you saw?"

"Marcus. I mean, I was sure it was him."

"Did you see this Marcus?"

He could see the uncertainty in her eyes.

"No. But it must have been him. I felt it was. I thought I saw Marcus out there. And he laughed. It was the same. It sounded the same as it used to sound."

She sat down again and put her head in her hands.

"And the laugh—you're sure it sounded like this man, Marcus?"

She looked up, rested her face against the cool glass of the window and closed her eyes, as if trying to recall the sound.

"No. It could have been any sound. It's just that I was afraid and I imagined —" She shook her head. "No. It wasn't him."

"This is the person who makes you afraid, this Marcus?"

She nodded her head, her eyes still closed.

"Emily. It wasn't him. It was an Italian thief—known to the authorities. It wasn't your Marcus."

"Not *my* Marcus. Never my Marcus. Not after what he did."

He had to turn away from her then because he suddenly understood. So it was this man, Marcus, who had committed such atrocities. With all the force and strength of his character, dredged from deep down, he held his tongue and turned back to her. She needed him. She didn't need his anger.

"*Cara*. Come here." He pulled her to him and gently cradled her head in his hands. "It was not Marcus. The man is gone. But I promise you this other man will never come near you again." She looked up at him. "I promise." He kissed her then, wanting to comfort and reassure but also needing to express the consuming tenderness he felt for her.

But she pulled away. "How can you promise? No-one can. It's down to me."

"Don't shut me out, Emily. I'm here now and here I'll stay." He looked around, noticing the flashes of light from the guards outside the window—the numbers having been doubled after the intrusion. "I'll stay with you but not here. The place is still virtually cut off. We have all the dispensation we need to move into the cliff-top villa. We'll stay there from now on."

"But what about the dig?"

He shook his head and smiled "You don't give up easily, do you? Don't worry. It can wait. It's going nowhere. But we are. We're going back to civilization."

EMILY SANK into the hot bath, sighed and closed her eyes.

Civilization certainly had its compensations. The Rovello city house—the house where she'd first met Alessandro, set high above the city on the cliff top—was as luxurious inside as it was out.

It must have been past five in the morning—she'd lost track—but she desperately felt the need to cleanse herself in piping hot water. She inhaled the scented water and felt the candlelight flicker behind her closed lids. The storm had blown itself out and there was nothing but silence now. She felt safe for the first time in years.

She opened her eyes at Alessandro's knock on the door. As she watched him walk over to her and sit down on the side of the bath, she felt the familiar surge of love that swept through her every time she saw him. But this time the heat of love had an added, poignant note when she saw the concern in his eyes and the drawn pallor of tiredness and worry in his face.

Silently he picked up a sponge, lathered it and gently slid it along her arms, and up to her shoulders, tracing the scars and bones of her back.

"Will you tell me how it happened?"

She closed her eyes tight. How to tell him what a fool

she'd been; how she'd somehow provoked such violence from someone who appeared so quiet, so in control? The psychiatrist she'd seen for years had taken her through a healing process of sorts. But she still couldn't quite believe that some of it wasn't her fault.

"He was my tutor at university."

She tried not to look at Alessandro's face but she felt the hesitancy of his touch before he continued to sponge her body.

"Go on."

"He wanted me."

"And you couldn't say no?"

She shook her head. She didn't trust herself to speak. But Alessandro was patient. She took a deep breath. "He was the first person who wanted me."

She felt his grip tighten. "Where were your parents? Your family? The people who should have protected you."

"I had none. They died. None of the remaining family could help so I was fostered out. First to one family and then to another. I was too old; too clever; too smart-tongued; and in a couple of cases, too able to look after myself."

"But your ability to look after yourself failed with Marcus?"

"Yes. Because he said he loved me."

"That wasn't so much."

She swept her arm across the water, spilling it onto the floor and turned to face him.

"You have no idea. How would you? Spoiled, as you've been, by an extended family from day one." She looked around. "I don't know why I'm telling you this. I've had enough." She stood up and stepped out of the bath.

He pulled her to him before she could move, pressing her soaking body to his and wrapping her in a huge, soft towel.

She tensed for only one moment before she leaned into him, absorbing his healing strength.

"I'm sorry, *cara*. You're right. I have no idea. But I can guess. I can guess that you were a very lonely, clever child, isolated by your brains and your strong-willed nature, vulnerable to the first person who professed love."

She breathed him in deep, gaining courage and hope from his understanding. "It was good at first. He helped me in my studies, told me how to climb the academic ladder. But then, I guess I took off. I did well. I got a tenured position and he didn't. I started to get a life that wasn't within his control. I didn't see it like that, then, of course. But others have helped me to try to heal the hurt."

"And have they succeeded?"

"I thought they had, before tonight. But somehow I doubt that it will ever go away now."

"It's a part of you, of who you are. Accept it. But, *cara*, you're not that young girl any more. You've moved on, except you've taken with you that experience. You can't not. No matter what people say. People's experiences change them forever. But they carry on growing, they don't stand still."

"Sounds as if you're speaking from personal experience."

He pulled the towel around her and turned away.

"Come. You must be hungry." His voice was suddenly gruff. But then he turned and smiled, pulling her along with him. "Food, Emily. The stuff you like, remember?"

She smiled for the first time. "I remember all the stuff I like." But her flirtatious words were tempered by the fear and pain of her experience; they came out more softly than she'd intended. She could see their effect in his eyes. The flicker of heat she'd intended to ignite was there, but also a tenderness she hadn't seen before. He simply looked down into her eyes, lifted her face to his and swept his lips gently, so gently, across hers before pulling her close to him. His arms held her in an embrace that, despite the strength of his arms, was more supportive than demanding. She lay her cheek against his chest, feeling and hearing his heart beat in her body.

Slowly, she sank more firmly against him and felt his arms tighten in response.

Slowly, she turned her face, inhaled his scent and felt her body quicken in response.

Slowly, his fingers spread round her back and down and she felt his heartbeat quicken. She lifted her head to his and saw eyes that were darker than before, wanting more this time.

Their lips met again in a kiss, still tender but deeper: a long, languorous kiss that confirmed the new connection she felt between them. She pulled away breathless. "And I'm hoping for a delectable dessert."

His eyes narrowed. "Ever hear of dessert first?"

"My favorite kind."

As their lips met again, the towel dropped from around her. He picked her up in his arms and carried her to the bedroom where he placed her on the large white bed. Then he stood back and looked at her. She stretched one arm out to him.

"Alessandro. Come. I want you."

"*Cara*. You will have me. But not yet. I want to make you come with everything in my power. I want to feel you, to taste you."

She couldn't have argued any further even if she wanted to. And she didn't.

CHAPTER 9

*S*he was in up to her neck.

Emily lay in bed watching the patterns of the sun reflecting off the swimming pool ripple and swirl on the bedroom ceiling. She felt weak, helpless. Gritting her teeth, she started to rise out of bed but sat back on the bed quickly.

Months had passed since the storm and along with it their need to stay at the villa. They could live where they wanted: alone or together. And they'd been together all that time, unable to get enough of each other. But always they'd been protected—apart from that once.

She swallowed in an effort to contain the queasy feeling that threatened to rise. No. Please no. She closed her eyes in disbelief as the thought that had been niggling at the back of her mind took shape once more.

She rose more slowly this time and walked to the bathroom and locked the door. Peering into the mirror, she thought she looked paler than usual. She'd been working hard since the road opened a month ago and her nights hadn't been exactly without activity. But she'd been the happiest she'd ever been. There was no reason for her pallor. Her face twisted as a wave of nausea overtook her.

She emerged from the bathroom shakily and looked down at Alessandro's sleeping face. She still couldn't believe he was her lover. She went to touch his face, but her finger hovered as it traced the lines of his brow, his jaw, his mouth, then she dropped her hand.

What if she were pregnant? How would a child fit into the here and now?

She closed her eyes. She knew. But she needed to know for sure.

Her gaze was drawn once more to the light that was seeping into the east. She needed to get to a pharmacy fast.

She quickly showered, dressed and slipped quietly out of the villa, picking up Alessandro's car keys as she went. There was no-one around. Everything was quiet. The bay was ruffled with a brisk breeze. She felt like one of the little fishing boats, bobbing in the choppy waves, pulled by invisible currents, at the mercy of forces far beyond her control.

Up to her neck? No. She was drowning, not just in love, but in a sense of inevitability as to her fate. She *knew* she was pregnant even without the test. She could feel the change in her body and in her emotions. She was adrift and helpless, shut out from a future with Alessandro by the secrets he held close. Whatever happened, one thing was sure: she'd never let her child down, would always give her, or him, the love and care she'd been denied.

But before she made any plans, she had to be sure.

"AND WHERE HAVE YOU BEEN, Signorina Carlyle?"

She jumped, feeling absurdly guilty.

His voice was gruff, angry even. He was standing looking out at the sea sipping an espresso.

"Just into the city. I needed to get some things."

"And in my Porsche."

"Yeh," she said breezily. "Cool car."

He gave an irritated sigh and walked back to the breakfast table, indicating she should join him.

"You have a problem with me leaving without permission?"

If he could be shirty, so could she. Had sleeping with him meant she had to check in with him first before she went anywhere?

She turned to him with the intention of giving him one of her glares. The early morning sun bounced off his curls and the unbuttoned shirt revealed his tanned chest with its darkly curling hair. He looked at her, over a cup of espresso, through narrow, dangerously sexy eyes. Her stomach flipped again, her irritation forgotten.

"I do. Come here."

His voice was still low but it was undeniably an order.

She raised her eyebrow and he countered the slight show of resistance by a barely perceptible shift of the head, both teasing and challenging.

She smiled and walked over to him.

"You called, my count?"

He pulled her down on to his lap. "What has happened? You look very happy."

She felt her smile slip slightly. She'd forgotten how perceptive he was. "And why shouldn't I be?"

He narrowed his eyes. "You have every reason to be happy, of course, after making love with me last night."

"Of course. Enough to make any woman happy." Her grin broadened at his arrogance.

"And hungry?"

"What do you think?" She closed her eyes as his hands

cupped her bottom and shifted her more intimately onto him.

"I think if you wriggle like that on my lap much more, breakfast will have to wait."

"Really?" She eyed him directly and wriggled provocatively once more.

He pulled her head down and kissed her deeply, his hands pushing up inside her shirt and expertly flicking open her bra.

His lips claimed hers once more and his fingernails dragged lightly around the fullness of her breasts until they reached their target.

She gasped and pressed her lips to his head so he wouldn't see her vulnerability as his mouth found her nipples and kissed, nipped and pulled until she couldn't take it any more.

Her breathing came hard and her hands caressed his head, his back, drinking in his freshly-showered smell, remembering the taste of his skin on her lips. She wriggled even more intimately, wanting nothing between them. She pushed her hands inside his shirt, reveling in the heat of his body and the friction of his hair against her finger tips, before she slipped one hand down into his trousers and felt the tip of his arousal.

He pulled away and looked into her eyes sternly. "Tell me. How are you feeling now?"

"I want you."

"And that, signorina, is how I felt an hour ago."

"That is *so* not fair."

"Who said I played fair? Come. Get dressed."

"No." Her hands descended once more to his jeans. "I want you."

"And you shall have me. Later." He picked her up and put her to one side, regardless of her semi-naked state. "And I suggest you get dressed properly before the staff arrive to clear the table."

She flushed red and pulled her bra down and slowly did up her buttons.

"Where are you going?"

"To work." He walked up to her and kissed her gently on the mouth.

"It's Sunday," she pouted. She hadn't known she could pout.

"Which makes it a perfect day for a site visit, without people showing me what they think I should be shown."

"You know what they say—all work makes—"

"And that is why I will have the car come for you at lunch time."

She crossed her arms. "I might just be busy."

He smiled and pulled her to him and gave her a long, lingering kiss. "Not too busy to play I think."

Her pulse rate had increased and her arousal would be betrayed if she spoke. She simply nodded.

"Umm, I thought so."

Suddenly the thought of him leaving filled her with fear: fear of the known, of the future without him.

"Don't go yet. Stay. Just a little longer."

He smiled, the smile of a man satisfied that he had the undivided lust of his woman.

"You want me to have you here and now?"

"And that would be bad because?"

"Have you no self control woman?"

"Rich, coming from the man who lives in the present—taking what he wants, devouring it, spitting it out and then moving on." She hadn't meant to be so plain spoken but the truth always seemed to have a habit of tripping off her tongue too easily.

He visibly blanched. "Is that how you see me?"

"That's how you describe yourself." She shrugged.

"You're correct, of course. And, it is something you should not forget."

How could she?

She had one more week of waiting before she knew for sure. She didn't want to see a doctor yet. She wanted the anonymity of a test—even if it was still inconclusive. It looked likely that she was pregnant, but not definite. The months she'd hoped for with Alessandro could possibly be only weeks.

She nodded, unable to disguise her pain so easily now.

She watched as he walked away. It was all she could do to hold herself back, not follow him to touch him once more. He turned at the door and smiled the lazy smile that drove her mad.

"And bring your bikini."

Her smile dropped. "I don't swim."

"Who said anything about swimming?" He turned and walked out of the door.

She moved slowly to the window and watched his Porsche roar into life and disappear out of sight in a cloud of dust. She continued to watch as that same dust settled, re-forming over the tyre tracks, their imprint now muted.

NAPLES WAS TEEMING with people enjoying its sunshine, food and exuberance. It was a day for flirtation with people of all ages thronging the streets, the bay, the restaurants. As the car slipped slowly through the busy streets she caught glimpses of other people's lives through the air-conditioned windows.

She watched transfixed as a beautiful young girl—surely no older than sixteen—sashayed past a group of older boys up to her equally young boyfriend. She watched as they kissed. She watched as they turned to leave the café. She watched as the girl turned back coyly, flirtatiously, to the group of young men and smiled at their lusty remarks before following the young man who held her tightly by the hand.

A young couple with children sat exhausted, pale in the bright light as their children played in the sand: the woman talking incessantly, the man yawning. When suddenly he looked at her and smiled, whispered unknown words and kissed her passionately on the mouth, only to be slapped playfully away; the woman no longer care-worn, but a young girl once more.

Love. There was so much everywhere. How come she'd never noticed it before? It transformed people—if you let it, if someone loved you back.

Emily dragged her gaze away from the window—from other people's worlds. She had her own world, her own life. And for today, she smiled, she would be with the man she loved.

The car pulled into the driveway of an exclusive restaurant that overlooked the bay. Her heart quickened when she saw Alessandro, leaning against the door, waiting for her, a slow grin spreading across his face. He opened the door for her and helped her out. He immediately wrapped one arm around her and kissed her on the cheek.

"Glad to see the prescription sunglasses are coming in useful."

She patted her new handbag. "I still have my old ones, just in case."

"In case you wish to irritate me?"

"Now, why would I want to do that?"

"I have no idea, Emily. But there is so much about you that I don't understand, that I don't attempt to predict your behavior."

"I'd say I was very predictable."

"Then you have no self-knowledge." He turned to her

underneath the portico, searching her eyes. "As I said the first night we met, your eyes hold secrets. But come, we do not talk of secrets on such a day. Only pleasure."

"Pleasure is all right by me." They walked out onto a private deck overlooking the azure sea, white-flecked and stunning. "This place is beautiful." She plucked some antipasti from the table and popped it in her mouth. "And the food is beautiful too."

"Yes. It's a special place. I thought my lover should experience some of the finer points of civilization."

She shivered at his possessive words. "Are you calling me a heathen?"

"You tear around in the dust and stones in shorts and a t-shirt, mud on your face, dust in your hair, digging up rocks. You eat whatever is put in front of you. You are equally amicable with everyone. You are a heathen and the worst kind of socialist. Without any discernment."

"And you are the worst kind of aristocrat, believing that there is only one way to view anything and that everyone has their place in society's hierarchy. Perhaps," she hooked her elbows on the railing and leaned back, aware of the effect on him of her low-cut dress, "you can tell me just how low mine is."

He stepped towards her, ran his hands along her arms and then gripped the railings either side of her elbow. His body was close but not touching.

"Very low. Scraping the bottom."

She had no choice but to kiss his smile away. But when she stepped back she realized she hadn't succeeded. It had curled into his predator's smile: one that revealed he knew he had his prey just where he wanted it.

"I think we'd better eat." She ducked under his arm.

"I think so. Or you will be eaten."

They entered the private dining room that contained only

one large table set with silver cutlery and silver and white china that glowed in the light reflected up from the sea. She hesitated before entering.

"Is this the right place? It looks like someone's drawing room."

"That's because it was. All the furniture, all the fittings are original to the villa."

"Really?" She wandered over to look more closely at a painting that hung over the marble fireplace. "Complete with family paintings. Someone obviously didn't have much affection for their family if they were happy to leave all this behind: to sell absolutely everything."

"Yes. My father was not impressed."

"What? Who sold it?"

"I did."

"It was yours? You sold it?" Emily shook her head in disbelief.

"The house was left to me by my grandparents. It was mine to dispose of so I did."

"Why? It's beautiful."

"It's a traditional family home. I have no use for that."

"But all the family's possessions—"

"Not all."

"Surely you want to pass them on to your children."

"No. As I said, I do not need a family home because I do not intend to have children."

Emily sipped her water carefully and replaced it on the polished wooden table before answering. "You don't intend ever to have a family."

"No. Never."

"And may I ask why?"

He sat back and looked at her consideringly.

"Because I have nothing to give a family and because they

have nothing to give me. It's lose-lose. So why would I want to?"

She shrugged. "It's what everyone wants, deep down."

"No. Not me. And surely not you. From what you've told me you've seen enough of dysfunctional family life to last a lifetime. Come, let's eat and then we will have an afternoon of pleasure to look forward to." He poured her a glass of water and raised his own glass of wine to hers. "To pleasure."

Despite the heat in his eyes, his words struck a chill chord and she shivered.

She raised her glass to his without answering. For what was there to say? He'd made his position abundantly clear. He clinked his against hers, his eyes narrowed. He wasn't smiling now.

THEY DIDN'T ARRIVE HOME until late afternoon when Alessandro led Emily down to the private beach.

The waves tumbled into the rocky cove as Emily watched Alessandro dive into the surf and swim strongly out into the bay. His body was something to behold: his tanned skin, the sun glistening on the water as it slipped over his muscular back, flexing with each lift of his arm as it pounded into the sapphire blue water.

She shivered slightly under the brisk wind, but it wasn't from cold. It was like a harbinger of the future: cold, alone, always looking on. Back to where she once was.

She drew her arms around her—in more of a gesture of comfort than for warmth—and closed her eyes beneath the glare that still managed to edge its way around her sunglasses.

His ardor suitably cooled, Alessandro walked out of the water and stood over Emily. She was wearing the bikini that he'd bought her. He'd ordered the skimpiest available for his own pleasure. He'd been right. While her breasts were deliciously full and spilled out around the tiny triangle, the rounded stomach and thighs and bottom were well-toned with all her hard physical work, but still sensuously curved.

Umm. He couldn't go swimming again. He'd been trying to restrain himself because all he could think about was Emily—not only of what he wanted to do to her, with her, but thinking about what made up the sum of this woman who dominated his thoughts, feelings and dreams.

He raised his hand and dripped cold water onto her breasts. Her eyes flicked open with the shock and her nipples peaked immediately.

He dropped down and lay on top of her, covering her hot body with his wet one. He stifled her squeal with a kiss that showed his intentions quite clearly.

He raised his head and let his eyes drink her in. Tanned skin, vivid green eyes, now hooded with desire; fine light brown brows fanning out beneath a broad forehead. He loved the shape of her head, perfectly regular; he loved the tilt of her chin, perfectly challenging. His lips slipped to her neck and he breathed in her fragrance. He felt himself harden even more.

With his teeth he tugged aside the tiny scraps of fabric to reveal the rich dark nipples that grew tighter still, anticipating his touch.

Lazily he flicked his tongue against one, then the other, watching as she arched her back, wanting more. He smiled. God, he'd never wanted a woman so much. Never had a woman been so sensitive to his touch, so willing to move her body in time to his.

He lowered his mouth once more to her nipple and took it fully, his body lowering onto hers as he heard her gasp with pleasure and felt her legs shift to accommodate him.

He moved his mouth to the other one, his whole attention absorbed in her breasts.

"No, Alessandro. What if someone should see us?"

"*Cara*," he murmured, "there is no-one. The cove is private and not overlooked. But, even if it were? I would not care. Why would you? Making love is the most beautiful thing in the world."

"But—"

He staved off her retort by slipping his finger around the top of her bikini bottoms, teasing her with his fingers. He felt her flutter under his touch and, as she lay back in surrender, he pulled them off in one swift movement. He couldn't take his eyes off her face, her closed eyes luxuriating in the sensations that his fingers created on her body; her mouth, red and swollen from his kisses, moist and slightly apart. He groaned, pulled his hand away and rolled over, laying down beside her. "Yes, of course you're right."

Laughing, he caught her hand as it came across to slap him and he gripped it tightly, weaving his fingers through hers before kissing her fist.

"I will get my own back on you, Alessandro."

He propped himself up on one elbow, still holding her hand tight within his own and watched her. "I will look forward to it." He could see the reflection of the clouds in her eyes, passing swiftly by overhead; he could smell the sun and sea and sand on her.

He trailed his hand lazily around her face, her scarred shoulders and arms and her breasts before dragging his fingernails lightly in a straight line down from her navel. He could feel her tense in anticipation beneath his touch.

"You should be the subject one of those mosaics."

She laughed. The sound warmed him.

"Yeh, right. Who'd want to look at me?"

"Yes, you're right. Certainly it wouldn't be proper in some

circumstances. Religious, for instance. We wouldn't want to stimulate people who shouldn't be stimulated. But anyone else? My Emily, you have no idea."

His Emily? Emily swallowed, trying to contain the hope that surged at his words. Just a turn of phrase. Keep it light.

"Oh, I have some. Now let's see. What pose would you give me?" Her stomach heated with desire under the scrutiny of his eyes. Her body was on fire for his touch but she didn't move. And nor did he: simply lay there lazily and blatantly looking at her body from under narrowed eyes. She tried to be cool but she knew the rapid rise and fall of her chest pushing up her peaked nipples, gave away how much she wanted him.

"Umm." He rose, walked around her, eyeing up her naked body from different angles. "Perhaps move one leg like so," he pulled one knee up and pushed it out slightly. "Good. But not prone. We don't want a passive goddess do we?"

She sat and propped herself on her elbows, her breasts swinging lightly with the movement.

"Good. But one more thing." Before she could stop him he dropped down to his knees and suckled first one breast and then another, drawing the nipples to the fullest extent. He stood back. "That's better."

She could feel a wash of heat strip through her body and pool moisture where his fingers had toyed only moments before.

"Since when have you had all the say in this?"

"I am the artist here, am I not?"

"In your dreams, count." She rolled onto her tummy. "How about this view." There was a brief silence and she drew up her knees, about to get up when she felt his hands come under her hips and pull her to him and the thrust of his hard penis enter her deeply. She came instantly with a cry of passion that rocked around the small cove.

145

. . .

DARKNESS HAD FALLEN and they were alone once more in the dining room. It was formal, the huge table set with silver and their plates filled by the butler before he'd tactfully withdrawn. The night had settled into the typical Naples night: warm and humid. The evening breeze sent the fine curtains periodically billowing and then skittering across the wall and floor.

After the passionate love-making of the day, the distance between them seemed artificial. It somehow made Emily nervous. It emphasized the differences between them, differences that didn't matter when there was just the two of them, alone, informal, intimate. She looked up at him wondering if he, too, felt the change. But when he answered her look, she looked away suddenly.

She was being stupid. It was what it was.

She wriggled in her seat, aware of sand in awkward places and looked up at him to find him looking directly at her, his smile indicating he knew the reason for her movement.

Was there nothing this man missed? Just the sight of his eyes feasting themselves on her, of his lips moist from his drink, made her inner muscles flutter in expectation.

She shook herself. This wasn't real. This was never meant to have happened.

"What is the matter, Miss M?"

She twisted her lips. How to begin?

"Is this too formal for you? I thought it would be nice for a change, to have some of the comforts of luxury between you and your beautiful body."

"Rather than sand, you mean?"

"Esattamente."

"It is nice. It's beautiful." She looked down at her plate and pushed some risotto around with her fork. She was still feeling out of sorts.

"So, if it's not the surroundings, why the frown?"

"Just thinking," she shrugged lightly, and took a rapid sip of water, "how crazy this is."

It was his turn to frown.

He gestured around the room and to her. "It is normal. What is so crazy?"

"You and me. You're of this world. I'm not. It might be normal to you but, to me?" She shook her head. "You know nothing about me."

"I know all I need to know."

She snapped her head up.

"*That*, is an arrogant thing to say. All you want to know about me is how I relate to you, now. What about me? What about my past?"

"I don't need to know about your past. I don't wish to know about your future. All I want to know about you is here, right now."

"And that's my problem."

She looked at his frown, now lowered even further. "Why?"

"You don't get it do you?"

"No, *cara*, I rather think I do 'get it'. You want more than I'm prepared to give. I've never told you anything different. I am only interested in the pleasures of the moment. *That*, is all I have to offer."

She took a mouthful of dinner, almost abstractedly, tricked by its aroma and the needs of her body. She could feel his eyes watching her closely.

"There, that is what I am talking about. Listen to your body, close off that clever mind of yours. Follow the desires of your body and we will be good together."

She dropped her fork immediately. "I can't live like that,

Alessandro. There's more to me, more to what I want than what my body desires."

He came and stood behind her, his fingers splaying over her shoulders. She closed her eyes as her body responded automatically to his touch. She could do what he said, she could suspend her mind, it was so easy at that moment. She could give herself to him and to pleasure.

But what then? What happens when they awoke from their pleasure? Nothing? To be dropped when the present became less pleasurable?

He dipped down and kissed her neck. "Good. Tell me about yourself. Tell me about your future plans if you care to. I will listen. Tell me about your past. What happened to your parents?"

She shrugged. It wasn't exactly the conversation she'd envisaged, but it was a start.

"They died. End of story."

"Not for you it wasn't."

"I had no other close relatives that wanted me and I wasn't the most obliging, amenable little girl in the world."

He laughed. "I can imagine. And your foster families?"

"Most were nice. All were poor. East London housing estates. The local comprehensive. And the library. That was my salvation. The place I'd run to."

"Which led you to archaeology. And to me. So what next? What about your future?"

"Alessandro! You're talking about the future. Are you feeling well?"

"I'm talking about your future, not mine."

She smiled. "After I've finished with the Aphrodite Mosaic I'll return to the university briefly and then on to Antioch."

"Antioch? And when will this happen?" His touch on her shoulders hesitated briefly.

"At the end of the summer, after I've finished up here."

"Ah." The word was uttered briefly as if he were suddenly aware that he was betraying a sense of relief. Gone by the end of summer. No need for unpleasant scenes; the affair would come to a natural end.

"Well, that brief run down of my history and future plans seems to have satisfied you."

She felt his fingers relax on her shoulders and slowly draw away. She almost held up her hand to keep him there— his withdrawal leaving her feeling naked. But she stopped herself in time and dropped her knife and fork onto the plate. She rubbed her forehead.

"And is that why you think I asked you, in order to satisfy myself?"

"Whatever. You're relieved that I'm going. That much is obvious."

He shrugged, cold and grim. "I am neither relieved nor sad. Why do women always try to read so much into something. Why do they not take the pleasure as it comes?"

"Well," her voice was quietly angry, "either you choose the wrong women, or perhaps pleasure, to them, is not a fleeting thing of the present. Perhaps their needs are greater than yours."

"It's a theory."

"An inconvenient one, no doubt, but probably true."

"Is that true for you?"

She stood up. "Confessional over for one day, I think. I'm tired. I'm going to bed."

"I will be with you shortly."

She hesitated. She should go now, while she had a scrap of self-respect left, before she got in any deeper. She should leave immediately.

But then she looked at him, at the heat in his eyes. And he touched her, his hands running around her shoulders as he dropped a kiss onto her neck. She felt him inhale her like a favorite perfume. And her resolve fled.

"Umm," he muttered. "A change of plan. I think it would be ungentlemanly of me to leave you to go to bed by yourself."

"How unselfish of you."

"Exactly. A man must look after his woman."

She closed her eyes briefly at the pain that his words induced. Knowing them for the truth and knowing their ephemeral quality. He meant it now, in this moment only.

And that should have been enough for her. But it wasn't just about her any more.

CHAPTER 10

*E*mily gripped the sides of the hand basin and studied the pregnancy test that was propped up under the mirror.

Nothing.

She was too impatient. She waited, watching to see if the thin blue line would appear. Her mind wandered to Alessandro. If she weren't pregnant, they would have more time together. She smiled to herself. What did the future matter if the present just went right on moving up into the future, without anyone noticing? She'd found her home—with him. Everything could be perfect.

She checked the pregnancy test again. No sign. Her heart leaped. She checked her watch. Not sufficient time had elapsed. She sighed, denying the wave of nausea that swept her. Too much rich food perhaps.

Antioch could wait. There was heaps of work she could do on the estate. Getting Alessandro's permission to go ahead would surely be a formality. To be with him, night after night, day after day, in his arms, being teased by him, being loved by him, was all she wanted. She caught sight of herself in the mirror, soft smile, dreamy eyes. It wasn't a face she'd ever known before. Her smile broadened. She'd simply have to get used to it. Because being with Alessandro, loving him as she did, had changed her.

Still smiling, she looked back down at the test.

The thin blue line had crept into place from nowhere, silently bringing with it changes Emily couldn't begin to comprehend. All she knew was that the vision of her home with Alessandro had just evaporated like a mirage: something created out of a distortion of reality, fading just when it appeared to be within reach.

She looked back into the mirror. Her face was blank, disengaged, distanced.

Time had just run out.

THE LATE AFTERNOON was still hot but, out on the deck overlooking the glittering sea, the breeze kept her cool.

She knew when he'd joined her on the deck. There was no sound. But she could sense his presence.

"You're late." Her voice no longer even sounded like hers. It was flat, unemotional.

"How do you do that? Know that I'm here when you haven't turned around?"

"It's a gift I have. It means that you can never find me unless I wish to be found." She turned around and looked at him like she might observe a beautiful film: interested, appreciative, but essentially untouched.

She watched his eyes narrow as he registered that something was different.

"Drink?" Without waiting for his answer she rose and walked to the table.

"Si." He sat down on the seat opposite. Not next to her,

weaving his arm around her shoulders like he usually did. "It's been a difficult day."

Emily poured Alessandro his usual whisky and ice and gave it to him. His eyes hadn't left hers. She noticed that he wasn't asking her what was wrong, wasn't showing concern or sympathy. His eyes appeared to express a resigned inevitability.

She sat back down. "So, tell me about your difficult day."

"Small talk, Emily? I thought you hated it."

"Sometimes it's useful."

He took a sip of his drink, his eyes hard on hers. "Useful if you don't want to say what you're really thinking or feeling."

She raised her eyebrows and tilted her head in acknowledgement of the truth of his statement. She focused on her drink, swirling her tonic water so the ice clinked against the glass in a rhythmic sound that cut through the silence.

He put his glass carefully on the table and sat forward, his elbows on his knees, his eyes still focused on her. "You want to discuss it?"

She shook her head. "No. Tell me about your day instead." She looked up at him then, over her swirling glass of effervescent liquid, willing herself to relax and smile. "Really. I want to know."

He sighed and his mouth pulled into a line of resignation. "My day? We've moved onto stage two of the site development."

"Stage two? And that's what's made your day so difficult?"

"You don't understand. The valuers will be on site next week."

"What valuers?"

"Your job is to excavate the site. Mine is to develop it."

"Not my site you don't." She jumped up. "What the hell are you talking about? Valuers? First I've heard. Why do you want the estate, the dig, valued for God's sake?" She spun suddenly on the spot. "Are you going to sell it?"

"No. Of course not. It's just for the paperwork. That's all."

"Well that's something. But I can tell you this for nothing. No valuer is going to set foot on my dig."

"Emily. It's not yours. Look, forget about it tonight. We have to attend my nephew's birthday party. My brother and his wife are expecting us."

"What the hell do you expect me to do? Come along quietly when you've just dropped a bombshell like that?"

"Yes, I do. Be reasonable. There are developments and then there are developments. I'm not going to do anything to jeopardize the current excavations. It's a large estate. And it needs to pay its way. But I'm not unreasonable. I believe in what you're doing. You'll just have to trust me on this one."

"No valuers, no developers are going to set foot inside the estate while I'm in charge of excavations."

"You are my employee, may I remind you. You will do as I require."

"And what about my proposals for further excavations?"

He looked at her briefly and raked his fingers through his hair. "We'll talk about it later. I'm sorry. It's been difficult, as I say. I didn't mean to be high-handed with you. Come. I've had enough business for one day. We have a weekend of pleasure ahead of us and I, for one, intend to make the most of it."

She hesitated before standing up.

"I'll come." How could she not? She knew it would be their last evening together. And then tomorrow? The divisions she could feel rending their relationship would widen further as they fought over the land. But, for tonight, she'd be his lover first and foremost.

"Good." He smiled ruefully, as if worried that she wouldn't come.

"I wouldn't miss a birthday party: balloons, clowns, cakes, games."

He touched her then. Swept back the hair from her face with a wistful look. "Unlike you, I doubt my nephew has ever had a party like that."

And nor have I, she thought to herself.

EMILY CAUGHT sight of herself in the floor to ceiling mirror windows as they entered the grand foyer of Alessandro's brother's house. She hardly recognized herself. She appeared to have lost weight, her face looked more angular, her hair and clothes a glossy contrast to her old self.

The person in the reflection looked right at home in the austere, modernist building, with its concrete floor, sheets of glass, chrome and stainless steel. She could see that kids' birthday parties wouldn't exactly fit in a house like this. Her old self wouldn't have either. She'd changed: become someone she didn't recognize.

The interior was straight from the pages of a glossy magazine, more built for style than living. No clutter, no disorder anywhere. She wondered, briefly, what it would be like to be so confident of one's future, so in control, as the inhabitants of this house obviously were.

She looked around for children. All she could see was beautifully dressed adults, clustered in groups. Then she saw one. A slight boy of around ten years old stood nervously by his father as the sophisticated chatter flowed around him. He looked as out of place as she felt. Poor kid.

She looked out to the garden. The sole relief to the house was the setting. Beyond the reception room, whose wall of windows had been retracted to make a seamless transition to the outdoors, the terrazza and pool gave way to a lush, semi-tropical garden. With Alessandro soon claimed by relatives and friends, Emily slipped her hand from his as soon as the introductions and polite interest were over, despite his remonstrances, and went outside.

The cooler air of the hills was refreshing after the heat of the city and, feeling suddenly tired, she sat on a concrete bench under a grandiflora magnolia whose white flowers filled the air with their lemon scent. She felt hidden and able to observe, unnoticed.

There were few people outside. Most were watching Alessandro's nephew receiving his presents. He opened them more with a look of duty than enjoyment: certainly more dutifully than she would have done, given the fact that there was scarcely an interesting one amongst them. The only gift that made the boy's eyes brighten was the present she and Alessandro had given him—a set of remote-controlled stunt vehicles. From the look on his mother's face, she didn't share the same enthusiasm for vehicles that could careen around the floor and flip from one side to another.

Then she shifted her gaze to Alessandro. She'd thought she was hidden but he was looking at her, oblivious to the fact that someone was talking to him. He always seemed to know where she was. Just as she did him.

She watched him walk over towards her and she felt the same buzz of attraction as the first time she saw him. She wondered if it would always be that way.

"Tired?"

He sat down and slipped his around her, pulling her close to his side.

"A little." She nestled into his shoulder and chest, relaxing under the bliss of his touch. "Also wondering what's wrong with these people. Don't they know how to treat a kid? Even the kid doesn't know how to act like a kid."

He laughed and bent his head to hers. "You can see why I had to leave my home, my family, now?"

He halted a passing waiter and offered the tray to Emily.

She shook her head. "Not hungry."

"Don't let those curves fade, Emily."

She smiled wanly. She couldn't tell him the real reason she was off her food.

"No chance of that. The curves will only grow I'm afraid."

"Curvier curves do not fill me with fear. Quite the contrary."

She slapped his hand down, as it threatened to touch the underside of her breast.

"I'll get you a drink instead. Wine?"

"Juice please."

She watched him disappear and stood up and stretched, her hands unconsciously fingering her stomach. When would it start to show? She had no idea—knew nothing of families, children. She had only her instincts to rely on. And they seemed to have failed her in her choice of mate. He'd made it clear he wanted no ties and what bigger tie was there than a child?

She watched him walk back into the house in search of a drink and wondered what it would be like to grow up in a place like this, surrounded by freakishly adult entertainment, impossibly valuable artefacts and ancient and grand estates.

Her musings were interrupted by a light tap on the arm as a slighter, blond version of Alessandro came to a halt beside her.

"Signorina Carlyle. At last I get to speak with you. Apologies for not welcoming you earlier, but my brother seems intent on monopolizing you all evening."

"Yeah, he kind of does that, doesn't he? You must be Giovanni."

Giovanni smiled, amusement filling his face. "Indeed. And yes, he kind of does. But I can easily see why in your case."

She raised an eyebrow in query. "Demanding, embarrassing, that kind of thing?"

He laughed. "Hardly. Wanting you all to himself I should imagine. My brother never did like to share his toys."

It was Emily's turn to laugh.

"He's not changed much then."

"Umm. In his taste in women, I think, he has."

She felt her smile drift from her face. She tried to halt it at her lips, but failed.

"Improved, no doubt." When filled with doubt Emily had always found it useful to show more confidence than she felt.

"Absolutely. You are very different to his wife."

His wife! A sickening blend of betrayal and pain slammed into her gut and drained her body of strength. She sat down before she fell down and shakily swept her fingers through her hair as if insisting on a control she did not feel. She swallowed hard, trying to keep the bile from rising, trying to keep the panic tight inside her. She'd never heard so much as a whisper about his wife. He was Emily's lover and yet he had a wife? She cleared her throat, aware that Giovanni was watching her closely and determined to give no-one the satisfaction of seeing her pain.

"How different?"

"Did you know her?"

She shook her head, unable to speak after that effort, unwilling to show her complete ignorance that Alessandro was married. But she noted the past tense and the barest thread of hope rose from nowhere.

"She suited Alessandro to start with. She was very beautiful and you know, I'm sure, how Alessandro needs to be surrounded by beauty."

"Of course." If Giovanni was trying to make her miserable he was going the right way about it.

"But then, there was little more to her than beauty. She

needed to be adored and her whole world revolved around that. And that is not something someone of Alessandro's integrity and intelligence could admire, or live with."

"So, he left her."

Giovanni looked at her sharply. "He hasn't told you anything about her or his son has he?"

She pushed her fingers against her throbbing brow, trying to erase the feeling that her world was crashing down on her. She shook her head.

"No."

"Then get him to. He's been hiding it for too long." He touched Emily on the shoulder. "I'm sorry if I shocked you with this news. But it is best you know and best if you talk to him about it. It's not good for him to bury these things." Giovanni looked over at Alessandro who was walking towards them and then he looked at Emily once more. "But you are—good for him, I mean. He needs to do what father brought him here to do. Face his past. And you need to help him because he's not going to do it alone."

Alessandro slipped his arm around her. "Giovanni, filling my lover's ears with family gossip?"

"You should tell her about Eva and Niccy, Alessandro."

Alessandro's eyes narrowed and his lips tightened, white. "It's nothing to do with Emily."

"Tell her." Giovanni wandered off, apparently unconcerned that he'd just left a storm in his wake.

"I'm just getting a little ticked off about all the stuff that has 'nothing to do with Emily'."

"Sit. You look pale."

She remained standing. "Are you going to tell me?"

The broad-leafed leathery tropical plants hung heavy over the swimming pool: as heavy as the atmosphere that now lay between them and as heavy as Emily's heart. The party continued but at a distance from them. She felt isolated like never before. Tears pressed at her lids but she refused to allow them to surface and refused to break the silence.

"OK. What do you want to know?"

"About your wife and child. Where are they?"

"Dead."

"Oh! I'm so sorry. I had no idea. The way Giovanni spoke of them, I thought that they simply lived elsewhere."

"No. Dead. Five years now."

"I'm so sorry," she repeated hardly able to frame a reply when her mind and emotions whirled with the implications of his words. She sat down. "How did they die?"

"You want to know all the details? OK then. I'd grown bored with my wife. There was nothing beyond her beauty and I'd grown tired of continually pandering to her needs— superficial and shallow. She'd taken a lover and the two of them were going to leave, providing I gave them sufficient money to start a new life with. And they used my son as a bargaining pawn. They'd take him with them unless I paid them in full. I hit the lover—repeatedly. My wife, erroneously believing I was about to do the same to her, fled with my son. They died the instant the car hit the tree. So there you have it. I am responsible for killing my own son."

"No!" Her shout made people look across at them, over the pool. "No. It wasn't your fault."

"Emily. It is not open for discussion or analysis. You wanted to know what happened and I've told you."

"And you've kept on running ever since," she said quietly, understanding creeping into place.

"I have no future without my son. Nothing can replace him. Nothing." The bitterness and deep, deep sadness shocked Emily.

"You can't say that. You're young, you will marry again, have children, whatever you say."

The coldness in his eyes shocked Emily further.

"I will never marry again. I will never have children. I couldn't take care of my son. I lost him. He is not a commodity to be replaced."

"But that's not how it is. That's not how it could be." Emily could feel the strain, the tension of her profound distress at seeing a possible future—albeit one that she'd already decided she couldn't have—taken away from her. Before, there had still been possibilities because it had been her choice. Now there were none. Alessandro didn't want to settle down and share his future with someone. Now she could understand why.

"Emily. Don't talk about what you don't know. Come, I have told you what you wanted to know. Let's go back to the party."

"Party, yes." She spoke as if she were a sleepwalker trying to shed the vestiges of a ragged nightmare. "A party without clowns. Who needs surprises, when we can bring our own?"

He looked at her strangely.

She was glad there weren't any clowns.

Alessandro took her arm and guided her across the garden, back to the house.

"Where are we going?"

"To meet my sister-in-law. At least she can be trusted not to gossip, unlike my dear brother."

She wanted to go home. But where was home? Alessandro evidently believed that his news was not enough to curtail the evening and so he introduced her to Daniela. Emily met the cool, suspicious, uncomfortable looks of Daniela and her friends with an expression that Emily knew was incapable of revealing anything. She felt too numb. Within minutes, Alessandro had make his excuses and wandered off, leaving Emily alone in the crowd, wondering where everything had gone wrong.

· · ·

ALESSANDRO LOOKED DOWN at her through the myriad reflections and windows that intervened between her and him. Even the distortions of perspective and reflections couldn't take away the knowledge that she'd decided to leave him.

It didn't need to be spelled out to him.

She didn't want what he could offer and so she was leaving.

He watched her as, bored with small talk, she turned away without noticing that her companion was still talking to her.

He watched her as she eyed a passing tray of food but turned, tray untouched and sipped her drink.

He watched her as her eyes strayed to his nephew and stuck there, watching him, oblivious to anyone else around.

She was like no other person with her strength of character, her ability to be herself amid the vacillations of others—not like his deceased wife, not any girlfriend, not any relation. But it wasn't her uniqueness that held him. It was the fact that he could feel her pain from this distance; he could feel her—everything about her—as if she were a part of him and he were feeling her emotions first-hand.

That was the difference.

But if that difference had a name, he didn't know it, couldn't form it on his tongue.

And until he could, he had to let events run their course. He might not like them but he was powerless to stop them. Because he had no *right* to promise her anything he couldn't deliver.

She'd decided to leave and he'd let her go. But not too far. He couldn't let her leave the estate yet. The thought was simply untenable.

IT WAS late before they got to bed.

The wind blew the curtains back and forth. It was quiet, black as pitch outside and Emily felt strangely peaceful, as one is when one makes a decision that has proved inevitable.

She hadn't known how to tell Alessandro about her pregnancy before. But now it was clear. She didn't need to. He wanted no more children, no more family, so what was the point? And if one thing was also clear to her it was that she wanted this child more than anything and she wanted him or her to be needed and loved more than anything. There would be no second-rate affection or foster home for her child. Her child would be loved by her birth parent.

They lay side by side silently.

It was the first time they hadn't made love the moment they were alone. And she knew what he was thinking and feeling.

He'd returned to the party later in the evening. And she watched as he talked and flirted his way around the room. She wasn't jealous, just hurting for him. Because she knew he was trying to drown the memories that had surfaced. She was now part of that past. She was no longer wanted.

Except his hand reached over and held hers in the dark. Neither could see each other's faces, only the shadows, the edges. But she could feel the heaviness of their souls.

He stroked her hand and his fingers tenderly moved up her arm and around her body. Still he didn't move.

Her limbs felt heavy but her body couldn't help but respond to his touch. Bitter-sweet, the sensations filled her body as before, but filled her mind as never before.

She had to leave. This would be their last night together. She couldn't hide the fact any longer that their "present" was ending. Her future was beginning—it was growing inside of her—and she needed to give him or her the best chance possible. Her future would be alone—with the child.

But she had tonight.

She closed her eyes to hide the pain of emotion that flooded her as his hand lazily trailed over her breasts and stomach, down to her sex. She gasped as he lightly played with her.

"Move closer," she whispered.

He rolled over onto his side so he was looking down on her, his hand resting gently on the curve of her hips.

"Alessandro?"

"Emily."

"Hold me. Please?"

He pulled her close and she could feel the heat and strength of his body pressed against her softness. She tried to enfold each touch, each sensation into the recesses of her memory so she could revisit it when he was no longer with her.

"Emily? Are you well?"

She nodded, smiling, her eyes still closed.

"Just tired." Her voice was cracked, parched as if unable to assuage her thirst.

"You wish to sleep instead of making love?"

"Not *that* tired." She squeezed her eyes closed, praying that the tears that pooled there wouldn't spill down her cheeks. Then she opened them.

She caught her breath.

His hair: her hand automatically rose to feel the strength of its curl, the silkiness of its texture; his eyes: brown-black in the dark, they reflected the light from the solitary candle. The passion in them tore at her heart.

How could she live without this?

Her finger traced his lips. His teeth nipped it as his hands gathered her body to him.

They lay looking at each other in uncharacteristic silence, their fingers and hands tracing each other's outlines, their skin, their bones, their muscle and sinew. She, determined to commit to memory every inch of him; he, sensing her removal, her distancing and trying to reduce it by his touch.

But she held herself mentally aloof—she had to—even while their bodies touched, even when he, gently, oh so gently, slipped inside her and filled her body with such sensations that should have eclipsed her thoughts, dominated her mind. But she couldn't let him go there. She needed somewhere safe.

They came with a flood of warmth and quiet that filled her with more longing. But she knew she could never fill that void. It was something she had to live with. Always.

MUCH LATER SHE sat and watched him. His face, so gentle and relaxed in repose. She loved the way he awoke. There was no transition period. It was a direct route from deep sleep to wide awake. Within the space of a minute he'd awoken and swung himself out of bed, reaching for his robe as he drew back the curtains. He narrowed his eyes as he surveyed her and her packed bag.

"You're leaving."

It was a flat statement. Succinct. A world lay within those words and yet they both knew that nothing further could be said.

"I've done as much as I can do here. You've other plans. I'm leaving for Cambridge today."

He grabbed hold of her hand. "No you're not."

"Alessandro!" She tried to pull her hand away but he held it too firmly.

"Leave me, if you must. But you will not break your contract. I need you."

"You don't need me."

"I want the mosaic finished, Emily. I won't release you until it's done."

165

He let go of her then and she walked backwards away from him, unable to believe that he would hold her to the contract after all they'd been to each other. In the doorway she hesitated.

"Alessandro. You can't mean this. I need to go. You must let me."

He shook his head. "If you leave the estate I'll sue you and your university. You are to finish the dig in accordance with your initial brief—no more, no less. And you must complete the mosaic."

Something died inside of her then. She felt it viscerally, pop, burst and disintegrate, without leaving a trace of emotion. She had nothing left now. She shook her head in disbelief and turned and left without a word.

CHAPTER 11

*A*lessandro checked his cell phone one more time, snapped it shut and sent it sliding across the desk. No message from Emily. He raked his fingers through his hair, and stood up, hands thrust into his pockets and glared across the bright bay.

Not a word from Emily, in any shape or form, for three months. And he refused to make contact with her. It was *she* who had left him. It was *she* who wanted more than he could give. All he could do was make sure she hadn't gone far and he was paying the price for his heavy-handed measures. She would have nothing further to do with him.

He'd known she was leaving for good. He could see it in her eyes, he could feel it in her body and he could sense it in her mind.

And worse than that, he knew why. Because he'd told her to go if she wasn't satisfied with what he could offer her—the here and now, no future, no promises. So she'd left and it had been his fault.

After the events of five years ago, he'd set his life on a course that had allowed him to manage his pain until he hardly felt a thing. And then she'd come along and opened him up to feeling again.

And he'd run and not had a moment's peace since.

He missed her. He wanted her more than he wanted to blot out the pain and guilt of the past. He wanted her more than anything else.

He turned away from the brilliant colors of the bay, not even noticing them. Life was drained of color for him since she'd left. There was nothing real to him about his surroundings without her. She brought life to his life. He had only one thought on waking and one on sleeping. Emily.

The dig was nearly complete. His waiting time was over. If he didn't go to her soon he'd have no further excuse to keep her.

He flicked a look at his watch and grabbed his car keys.

It was late afternoon when he arrived at the estate.

The place was now teeming with not just archaeologists but also the surveyors who were marking out where the new buildings would be erected. It was late and they were packing up for the night.

He looked over and saw the remains of the archaeology team resting in the shade of the huge trees. The team had dwindled down to three, including Emily. But there was no sign of her.

"Where's Emily?"

The boy and the girl exchanged looks. They hesitated and he pushed his glasses to the top of his head so that they could see with whom they were dealing.

The girl shrugged. "Try the mosaic. She spends most of her time there now."

He nodded. "You've finished here for today."

"No, not yet."

"It wasn't a question."

He waited until everyone had gone and walked slowly through the site. It still remained uncleared, awaiting the completion of the archaeology. He'd had his architects revise the plans in line with Emily's vision. He'd been right to make the changes. It would prove a significant point of difference —a huge selling point—for his exclusive resort.

He walked along the now uncovered mosaic that led to the Aphrodite Mosaic. He stopped in the shadows of a fig tree. Emily was standing, unmoving before the mosaic. He hadn't seen her in months and was shocked by the changes he saw in her.

She was thinner, much thinner, and full of nervous agitation. Her brows were compressed in a deep frown as she stood looking at the mosaic. Her fists clenched repeatedly around whatever she was holding before she suddenly turned and paced away. Then she paused once more in front of the mosaic, impatient fingers plucking at the shapeless shirt that hung down from shoulders tight with tension.

His heart pounded and his hand clenched a branch of the tree, oblivious to the thorns digging into his skin, in an attempt to stop himself from going to her immediately. Something terrible had happened.

She turned as she heard the others leaving across the estate. Shouts of goodbye, laughter receding, cars revving and then silence.

She dropped the pieces of tesserae she'd held in her hands, grunted with frustration and drove rigid fingers through hair that was already disheveled, revealing the turmoil that raged within. Then she slumped down onto the ground and sat staring at the incomplete mosaic.

Dio! What had he done?

He'd told her he'd look after her. And he hadn't.

He took a deep breath and was about to step forward when she arched her back and winced. Her stomach pushed out, clearly revealing that she was pregnant.

Stunned, he stepped back further under the shelter of the tree, pressing himself against its trunk. Pregnant! But how? Then he remembered the one time when they'd made love unprotected when she'd turned up at the party to make a point, revealing her bare shoulders. He'd been angry with her and it had come to this? Of all the times they'd made love, that time was not the one he wanted to remember. But now he was forced to face up to the consequences. But could he?

He sank down to the ground and continued to look at her, looking at the mosaic.

He'd avoided facing up to his past for years. And that was fine because the only person he was hurting was himself. But now? It wasn't about him any more. It was about the strong, independent woman who now looked desperate and despairing. She needed him and he could no more turn around and leave her than not breathe.

He stepped forward and cleared his throat.

Her reaction was instantaneous. She jumped up and swung to face him, pulling out her shirt once more to hide her stomach. Clearly she didn't want him to know. And he'd wait for her to tell him.

"What do you want?"

He felt the depth of anger and frustration in her words but they were no match for his own.

He stepped towards her and stood, close but not touching.

"To see you."

"You've seen me now so you can go."

He reached out and tried to lift her chin to force her to look at him. But she stepped back and looked away, firm and resisting. But this close he could see just how changed she was. The last of the light caught the planes of her face, creating shadows beneath her eyes and cheekbones where there was no longer any softness.

"You've been ill. Are you going to tell me about it?"

A cynical smile rested on her otherwise impassive face and she shook her head in one jerky movement of denial which told him more than words.

With a faint grimace she bobbed down and picked up some trowels, banging them together to rid them of dirt, her face unsmiling now. It seemed to him that he'd never seen her without a smile, without some kind of animated expression on her face.

"I'm fine." She cleared her throat, as if she hadn't spoken to anyone for a while. "Never better. Come to see the progress?"

He stepped away, instinctively, as if struck. He could feel the chill of her words as if they were solid objects pelting his body.

He looked away from her then. "Progress?"

"Is it to your satisfaction?"

He wanted to cradle her in his arms, to shake her, to make love to her, to turn her back into the woman whom he... He stopped himself there because he knew no word to finish the sentence. All he knew was that he wanted her old self back.

He forced himself to approach the mosaic.

"It's incomplete." He paused. What could he do to jolt her back into being his Emily again? He had to be hard. If she wouldn't take his caresses, then he had to force her into a corner where she had to come out fighting. "That's not what I'm paying you for."

What he hadn't expected was for the jolt he wanted his words to make on her, to have the same effect on him. He knew he had to continue but felt the pain he was inflicting on her, on himself also.

She turned away. Her hurt was palpable. But he had to reach her so he continued.

"You have all the missing pieces. It simply has to be reconstructed. What's stopping you? We need it for the centre-piece of the building."

"So I understand." Her voice nearly broke him up. It had a light-hearted quality as she tried to distance herself from her pain.

"Well then?"

She cleared her throat. "You need to get yourself a new archaeologist."

"You're the best."

She turned to him then and for the first time he saw her eyes—made huge by her now delicate face—and caught a glimpse of what lay behind that agitated, brittle exterior. The look of despair cut him to his heart. "I *was* the best."

"What's changed?"

She shrugged. "Don't know. Me, I guess. It's just not working." She looked at him again with those eyes that could conceal nothing from him. "You need passion for this job. And I've lost mine."

He shook his head. "Not you. You've more passion than anyone I know." Again the bleak look. "How did this happen? Tell me, Emily." She looked so devastated that he began to think there was something more. Fear entered his heart then. "Is there something else? Tell me!" He could hear his voice shouting but he didn't care. "Were you scared of Marcus?"

She turned and began to walk away and he followed her, desperation taking over.

"You shouldn't have been," he continued. "He died two years ago. I checked."

She stopped instantly. Slowly she turned around. It was as

he hoped: the desperation had given way to anger. "You checked and you didn't tell me?" Her voice vibrated with barely concealed anger.

"The proof didn't arrive until after you left. I'm sorry. But if that's what's getting to you, there's no reason for further concern. I'd made sure your team moved in with you when I wasn't there. I made sure you were OK."

"How could you?"

He shook his head and tried to gather her hands into his. "How could I what? Tell me."

"No!" She shook his hands away. "No, Alessandro. It wasn't Marcus. He was a ghost but a ghost that you drove away. That isn't the reason that I'm..."

"You're what Emily? Is it the development?"

"Not even that. You were right. It's not going to be so devastating. I was being precious. It will be fine. Not exactly as I wanted, but with the changes you've made, it will be fine."

The trowel slipped from her hands and landed with a metallic clang as it hit the mosaic.

He looked into her eyes for a moment, testing her. But he had to go further, haul her out of the depths of despair into which she'd sunk.

"Mind the mosaic."

"You bastard!" That was better. "You mind the bloody mosaic. It's you who's after perfection, it's you who wants to use it to impress, to sell, to fund your future project. You mind it."

"It's your job and you haven't completed it to my satisfaction." He walked over to the Aphrodite Mosaic and crouched down beside it. "Why isn't it finished?" He shot her a quick look, trying to gauge her reaction. At least anger was an improvement on the despair that was too devastating to contemplate.

He saw the pain re-enter her eyes but it was too late to go back.

She came and knelt beside him, her hands hovering over its bumpy surface, but not touching it. She pulled away her hand before it came into contact with it.

"I can't."

"You must. It's to be the centre-piece of the development."

"Use one of the others. I'm sure it can't matter much to you which collection of old rocks slung together is your centre-piece. Certainly won't matter to any of your wealthy clients. They'll be too busy indulging in eating and drinking and fornicating to notice anything very much."

"It's the Aphrodite Mosaic I want. It's the most perfect."

"Of course."

"There's little more to do. I'm surprised you haven't finished it."

He could see that she was close to tears and that she was determined not to break down again in front of him. She turned away briefly, looking around the site as if saying goodbye.

"I can't."

"I want it completed before you go. If you have some specific, logistical problem, tell me and I will sort it."

"No. I mean that I, I haven't been *able* to."

He came and put his arms firmly around her. "Emily. I don't know what's going on but tell me what I can do to help."

She jumped up as if she'd been shot through with an electric charge.

"Nothing." She looked away and then turned to him once more. "Yes, there is something. I left some reference material at the house. Get it for me and then I should be able to finish it."

"Sure." He stood up and made as if to hold her again but she stepped away.

"Just get it."

"Sure. Wait here. I'll be an hour. No longer. Wait. And we'll do it together."

He backed away, filled by an uneasy, nameless feeling but knowing she spoke the truth. He remembered checking on the folder after she'd left, thinking she probably needed it but holding on to it as if it were a lifeline. Waiting for her to come back to get it. But she never had. So it was important after all.

"Wait," he repeated. And then he turned and ran through the darkening estate.

SHE STAYED FOR TEN MINUTES, feeling the silence of the past engulf and strengthen her. She pulled her old shirt more tightly round, cringing at the thought of how near Alessandro had come to detecting her pregnancy, now too advanced to go undetected except by wearing her baggiest of clothes.

Did he know?

No. He would have run a mile if he'd noticed.

And he wouldn't get another chance to find out because she'd be gone before he returned.

She tried one last time. She picked up a piece of wheaten-gold tessera and placed it where she knew it went. Her hand hovered and then dropped. First one tear fell and then another. Shaking with sobs she fell against the thick wall and slid down onto the cold floor and turned away from the blood-stained sky.

She'd be gone before he returned because there was no way she could explain to him that it would break her heart to fit the last pieces, only to find it wasn't perfect; that all that work, all that time, all that thought and feeling, had created something that was still scarred, still flawed.

It was quiet when he returned to the estate. No-one around. No sound. No Emily.

She was gone just like he knew, deep in his heart, that she would be.

He walked through to the mosaic.

Unfinished.

She'd broken her word. She'd left before she'd finished it.

Not only that, but he could see that pieces had been removed that had been already placed into position by Emily. For it had only ever been Emily who had been allowed to touch the mosaic.

It was as if she couldn't bear to see it complete. As if completion wouldn't be enough. But what was it she wanted? Perfection?

He winced with the pain of realization. Of course it was. And she would never be enough in her eyes. He'd made it clear to her that she wasn't enough in his.

He closed his eyes and, for the first time, felt himself breaking with the echo of her pain, splintering with her emotion. He felt as if the barriers around his heart were disappearing and his heart was contracting and expanding, surging into a life of intensity and pain. He leaned his head against the cold, rough wall, and felt himself flooded with his love for Emily. It had always been there but he'd been too scared of the pain before; too scared that he wasn't enough to handle it, that he'd break anything that he held dear.

But what had this made him do? What had he done to her? He'd broken her down as effectively with his rejection as he would have done with his love.

He thumped the mosaic and turned away, flicking the

light on his cell phone to check the time. There could be only one place where she was going at this time of night. And he had a few friends who could help him out there.

THE AIRPORT WAS QUIET. The mid-week flight to London was the last of the night and wasn't in high demand.

Emily hugged her travel-stained holdall closer to her stomach and stared across the half-empty terminal, its bright electric lights, garish and draining. She always travelled light, even if that meant leaving things behind. And she'd left a lot behind on this dig.

But she was taking something much more precious away with her. Her fingers spread out around her rounded stomach.

It was cold in the air-conditioned departure lounge; the air conditioning still pumping out cooling air in the late evening.

Suddenly the doors behind the departure gate swung open but Emily stayed where she was. Let the others board first. She closed her eyes, trying to hold back the nausea that still lingered with her pregnancy and that was exacerbated by lack of food and a deep feeling that she was leaving too much behind this time.

"Signorina Carlyle?"

She nodded.

"Please come this way."

She raised her eyebrows. She had no aversion to boarding first. She followed him to the departure gate. "What's this about?"

He shrugged his shoulders. "I've been told to show you to a different lounge."

She narrowed her eyes. But before she could remonstrate he'd opened a door that led into the first-class lounge—now completely deserted apart from a lone figure, standing waiting for her.

Automatically she pulled her jacket tighter around her.

"Alessandro! My flight leaves in half an hour. You'd better be quick."

He turned to meet her, his eyes coolly assessing her face. "I'll take as long as I like. You won't be on that plane."

"I will."

"No. I've cancelled your seat."

The cry emerged from nowhere as she flung down her bag in a rage.

"What the hell do you want from me? Stop! Just stop it."

"I want you to do as you promised. Finish the contract."

"I can't."

"You can and you will."

"Alessandro." Her hands unconsciously caressed her stomach, her words emerging in a whisper: strained and tense. "Have you no mercy, no kindness in you?"

"You will have the appropriate resources this time. Come, the car's waiting."

She didn't have the energy to argue—both mentally and physically she was drained. She felt the firm grip of his arm and hand around her shoulders as if he didn't trust to let her go, as he steered her outside and down the steps to the waiting car.

IT WAS past two in the morning by the time they reached the estate. She stumbled out of the car, too tired to think. But instead of going into the house, he took her arm and led her across the garden to the dig.

"Are you crazy? I can't do it now."

"You must. There's no time left."

There was no-one there; only one lonely floodlight illuminated the part of the mosaic that was incomplete.

"Come." He picked up a piece of waiting tessera—they were all lined up, *not* how she'd left them—and gave it to her. The mortar was wet and waiting. "Put it in."

"Why? What's the point?"

"We both need to complete this thing." He took her shaking hand, covered it with his own and guided her hand until it was close to the mosaic. "Where does it go?"

"Here," her voice was unsteady.

"Then put it there."

They pushed it into place together.

He picked up another and, again, guided her hand down to the mosaic, before halting, waiting for her to place it where it should go. She wanted to resist his pressure but the larger part of her wanted to use her knowledge and submit to the instinctive need to complete the mosaic. And that same part allowed herself to lean against him, to take the strength he was offering her.

He picked up another. And another. With each piece the urge to resist lessened. And slowly the last few pieces came together.

She sucked in the night air sharply as the last piece was fitted. She wiped the tears from her eyes with the heel of her hands so she could see it clearly.

"You've got what you wanted. Look at it." Again her deep intake of the fragrant night air turned into a light sob as she tried to hold back the pain. "It's all wrong."

"You guided the pieces into place. You knew where they all went. It's not wrong at all."

"Just look at it." Her voice was quiet, jagged with emotion. "It's damaged. Can't you see? It's damaged and it always will be. It will never be perfect."

He turned her around to face him then. It was as if she'd said something that he'd been waiting to hear.

"*Cara*, you need to see." One by one he turned on all the floodlights until the whole room was bright as daylight with the mosaic in the centre. "It's whole. That's all we can do. Nothing is flawless but that doesn't mean it's any less beautiful. Open your eyes, mio tesoro, don't you see?"

She rubbed the tears out of her eyes, trying to see through the mist of a deep insecurity she hadn't even known she possessed. At first all she could see were the lines, the dark dividers that savagely interrupted the whole and distressed its beauty. She shook her head.

"No. Look at the whole thing." He pulled her away until she could see the mosaic as it was intended, lending the room a grace, an elegance and a beauty that had drawn her to it in the first place. "The scars will always be there. But scarring makes us stronger, remember. Not weaker. And there's perfection in strength. There's a future in that strength."

She shook her head, not in disbelief, but in awe as she truly saw the mosaic for the first time. But Alessandro must have misunderstood.

"Please, Emily," his voice cracked, "understand."

"I do. I think I do. It's just that I so wanted it to look new, untouched, flawless. And it's not. But I can't change it, can I? And, perhaps, I shouldn't, even if I could."

"It is as it is: beautiful in its own right. Like you."

He sank his face into her hair, his forehead resting on the top of her head and she could feel the struggle he, too, was going through.

"I'm so sorry, Alessandro, you tried to tell me that it's my own stupid self-image that stopped me from believing in myself."

He half-laughed and she felt him shake his head against hers. "I would not have dared to call you 'stupid'."

"Perhaps you should have done because I have been." She clasped his face between her hands and pushed him away from her so she could see him. "I'm letting it go, all of it, the scars, the fear. I don't want it any more. I'm so tired of it. It was hidden away so deep inside that I hadn't even realized what I was feeling, what I was doing." She looked at the mosaic, complete and brilliant under the bright lights. "But now I do; now it's clear."

"You would have realized sooner if it hadn't been for my own blindness and selfishness. I'm so sorry. Please, stay with me, make a future with me."

She closed her eyes tight. Everything was clear now. Everything. Including the fact that it wasn't enough to build a future on.

"I'm sorry, Alessandro, the answer's 'no'."

He reeled back as if she'd hit him. His face was ghastly under the bright lights. He shook his head. "You can't mean it."

"I do. You've held me now. You know I'm pregnant. But my child deserves more than a sense of duty. I know you're a man of your word. But I don't want you like this."

"Emily, don't you realize what I'm saying?"

"Of course I do. You see the future through our child. It's because I'm pregnant, isn't it? You don't love me, you've always been clear about that."

He laughed aloud with relief.

"You are one crazy woman. Why would I chase you around Italy, bring you back here, if I didn't want you, if I didn't love you?"

"Why wouldn't you say you loved me, if you did?"

He pulled her to him.

"Because I'm stupid. I love you, Emily. Marry me." He pulled her close until her stomach nestled into his body. "Keep me warm, keep me grounded, keep loving me like I love you." He kissed her hair, her cheek her lips. "Give me many babies, keep eating, keep laughing, keep enjoying life. Marry me because I want to share your life with you. Because I can't live without you."

Tight against each other Emily felt her stomach—her new life—press into Alessandro, his warmth filling her body. She could feel his heart beat under her cheek, vibrating through her body and finding its rhythm with her own. She looked up into his eyes, their brown depth illuminated by the white glare of the floodlights: full of love, full of promise for the future.

She nodded once briefly and watched as his eyes flickered with hope and then concern.

"Is that a 'yes'?"

Exhausted, she closed her eyes. It was too much looking into his eyes, knowing what he'd done for her and all that he promised. She nodded once more and leaned against him, her skin receiving his breath against her cheek, as necessary to her as the air she breathed.

"Yes?" He asked once more.

She tilted her face up to his and their eyes met in a communion that needed no words. She opened her lips to form the word he was seeking but her answer was no longer required and disappeared into a kiss that sealed their future.

EPILOGUE

*T*welve months later...

Emily peeped out from behind a tree, waiting for the music to begin. Alessandro stood in front of the Aphrodite mosaic, framed by the tall trees reaching up into the turquoise sky. In front of him their friends and family stood, also waiting. She felt a flutter of nerves and drew in a deep breath of crisp winter air, overlaid with the scent of orange blossom from her bouquet. The solo violinist began to play. It was time.

She stepped forward, glanced at Ophelia, asleep in her nanny's arms, before smiling briefly at their guests. Then she looked at Alessandro and that was it—no-one else existed. Dimly she was aware of the swish of her long white dress as it swept over the uneven tiles and the sounds of the violin vibrating across the intimate space. She quickened her step to be with him and he reached out, took her hand and brought it to his lips. "You look beautiful," he whispered as she took her place opposite him.

As they exchanged their wedding vows, Alessandro

continued to hold her hands tight within his, his eyes never leaving hers. She could see his love for her in their dark depths and, from the smile that flickered on his lips, knew that he was equally aware of her love for him. She had no nerves now, no insecurities, only an overwhelming sense of happiness. Before she knew it the ceremony was over and Alessandro's hands cupped her unveiled face and he kissed her—long and slow. Her body, her heart, her soul, melted into him and it was only when the cheers of their friends and family filtered through to them that they pulled away and Alessandro brought his arm tight around her, as if he were never going to let her go.

With Ophelia being carried in her nanny's arms immediately behind them, they walked along the narrow path towards the villa where the reception was to be held. The estate was still untouched by developments of any kind— Alessandro had seen to that.

"The estate looks beautiful, Alessandro. Just beautiful. I never imagined you'd keep it like this."

"You're not the only one." He held a dangling vine out of the way for Emily. "Of course, it won't make me any money."

"No, but it will make you lots of friends."

"Friends?" He glanced around at the crowds of guests who followed them. "I don't *need* more friends."

"Then why did you decide to keep everything just as it is?"

"There is only one reason I do anything, any more, Signora Cavour."

She raised an eyebrow and a smile tugged at her lips. "And that is?"

She knew. He'd told her so many times that she already knew his answer, but she never tired of hearing it. She watched the familiar smile settle on his lips as they walked out into the open garden lit by the warm red glow of the late afternoon sun. The newly renovated villa—their home—stood before them in all its glory. He paused and touched her cheek gently with his finger—it was all it took to command her complete attention.

"The reason for everything I do?" He shrugged and tried to look nonchalant but she recognized the teasing sparkle in his eyes. "Fame, of course. I'm famous, or rather infamous, for passing up such a lucrative opportunity."

She huffed in mock indignation as his hand slipped down her arm and gripped her hand. They walked across the lawn, while people fanned out from behind them and rejoined them as they advanced up to the loggia where the wedding feast was laid out.

"That's not what you've said before. Just yesterday you said—"

"What did I say, mia tesoro? That *you're* the reason for everything I do? That *you're* the center of my universe now? That nothing has meaning without you? Is that what I said?"

The familiar heat of his love spread through her body. She sighed. "Could be. Something like that. Not sure. Perhaps you need to tell me again."

He shrugged and turned away. "They're just words. You don't need them."

"I might do."

"No, you don't."

"Alessandro!" She tugged his arm.

"No," he repeated as he pulled out the chair for her to be seated. He dipped his head close to hers, until the warmth of his breath tickled her ear. "I will *show* you. If it takes all night, I will show you that *you* are the reason for everything I do. If it takes a lifetime of nights and days, I will show you, by my actions, how much I love you."

She swallowed back her tears. "Now, that, il mio amato marito, is my idea of perfect."

~

THE END

Dear Reader,

Thank you for reading *Perfect.* I hope you enjoyed it! Reviews are always welcome—they help me and they help prospective readers decide if they'd enjoy the book.

The **Italian Lovers** series continues with book 2, Her Retreat (also published as *Seduced by the Italian),* an excerpt of which follows.

My other series include **Desert Kings** and **Sheikhs of Havilah** which features sheikhs who are used to their every command being obeyed. Problem is, they fall in love with strong women with minds of their own. Their 'happy ever afters' aren't easily achieved, especially when you add a dash of mystery and intrigue.

The **Mackenzies** series and **Lantern Bay** series are both set in New Zealand. Against a backdrop of beautiful New Zealand locations—deserted beaches, Wellington towers, snow-capped mountains—the Mackenzie and Connelly families fall in love. But again, expect some twists and turns!

You can check out all my books on the following pages. And, if you'd like to know when my next book is available, you can sign up for my new release e-mail list here, or via my website —dianafraser.com.

Happy reading!

Diana

HER RETREAT (ALSO PUBLISHED AS SEDUCED BY THE ITALIAN)

BOOK 2 OF ITALIAN LOVERS—LUCA AND ISABELLA

An emotional romance that pulls at the heart strings.

Interior designer Isabella, Contessa di Sorano, is skilled at creating beautiful facades that cover a multitude of sins, especially when it comes to herself. Behind her immaculate appearance she hides a heart-breaking secret she's determined to keep. But when she's forced to sell the Castello Romitorio and accept a lucrative contract from her ex lover, she can no longer avoid facing up to her painful past.

Seven years earlier, Luca Vittori had been rejected by Isabella and he'd left Italy. But now he's back to honor a promise he made to his grandmother to hire Isabella to redecorate the castello. He just wants it over and done with so he can return to his home in Australia. Trouble is, he hadn't planned on re-igniting a passion he'd hoped was long dead—a passion which threatens to destroy before it can heal...

Excerpt

It was the draft of cooler evening air that first alerted her to his presence. A chill wave of alarm swept through her body as she snapped open her eyes to see the figure of a man standing in front of one of the large stone-framed windows. The saffron rays of the evening sun shone directly behind him, lighting up the motes of dust he'd disturbed and illuminating only his silhouette: shadowed face turned toward her, broad shoulders, elbows jutting as he thrust his hands into his trouser pockets.

"What the hell are you doing here?" Her voice was hoarse as if forced through a filter of raw emotion.

"I've come to see you." His voice was deeper than she remembered.

With his face partly in shadow, she couldn't see his expression. She didn't *want* to see his expression. Awkwardly she looked down and then away, out of the window, anywhere but at him. "Well, you've seen me. Now perhaps you'll leave."

He walked up to her and she felt his presence

encroaching on her space as much as his physical body. Both were more than she could deal with.

He stopped immediately behind her. "Are you ever going to look at me?"

"And why would I want to do that?"

"It's usual."

She turned slightly toward him, her head still lowered, unwilling to reveal anything to this man who had once meant so much to her; the man who had been instrumental in bringing disaster to her and her family.

"It's usual to be on time for your grandmother's funeral. It's usual to be with the woman who'd raised you when she's dying. It's usual to have kept in contact with her over the years. I think you have no sense of what is, and what isn't, usual."

She twisted in her seat and slipped her shoes back on her feet. Her hand trembled as she smoothed her already smooth hair, checking its length was intact in the perfect, low knot.

"*Cara*, I've long since come to believe that nothing is usual. Least of all my life, least of all yours."

His voice had softened, had become a caress that melted something she'd frozen long ago. She looked up at him then and what she saw wasn't what she'd expected to see.

While his clothes were immaculate, he looked tired and disheveled. Stubble darkened his chin, his black hair was too long and fell away from his face in rough waves and his honey-brown eyes were underscored by dark shadows. But it was his eyes that drew her. They hadn't hardened like she'd anticipated but still held the same passion and fire she remembered, except now the heat was tempered with a maturity and sadness she'd never seen before.

She barely saw the boy she'd once known in this man; he was broader, more powerful than she remembered. But she *felt* he was the same: it was the same feeling his eyes gave her when she looked into them; it was the same sensation of wanting to close the gap between them, that his body gave. Her eyes stung with heat and pain.

She saw from his reaction he'd registered her unwanted emotions. His frown lifted and the brown of his eyes darkened with the unmistakable flare of desire. He pulled his hands from his pockets and started forward, as if to reach for her. She held up her hand to stop him and looked away, shifting back against the window. She had to stop this. She needed to protect herself. She took a deep breath and faced him again, prepared this time for the onslaught of emotional turmoil that just seeing him, feeling him close, brought to her.

"You're wrong, Luca. Come on, tell me, why are you here? You failed to be with your grandmother during her last days and almost missed her funeral."

"I had no choice." His voice was quiet, contained by a tension in the tight lines around his mouth.

"Right. Something else came up more important than your grandmother. Business, no doubt. You've become your father, just as my father predicted. Business above all else. Why bother to come at all?"

His eyes narrowed dangerously—just as they used to whenever he spoke of the father who'd deserted him—and his jaw clenched as he worked at controlling the anger her words had evoked. But it was a relief to see some emotion other than the heat of desire in his eyes.

"As I said, something else came up. My grandmother knew about it."

"Your grandmother knew? Come on, you haven't seen her in years."

"I kept in contact."

"She didn't say anything."

"Perhaps she didn't tell you everything. Why should she

tell you about my calls, my visits? You'd made it clear you felt nothing for me, wanted nothing further to do with me."

She had. But, despite that, she felt a flicker of betrayal at her old friend keeping this from her; allowing her to think that Luca hadn't cared enough to see her.

"Of course. It's none of my business anyway. But it still doesn't explain why you're here, now."

"To see you; to talk with you."

"There's nothing to talk about."

He exhaled roughly and walked away, his quick gaze scanning the room. "I knew you'd be here. I watched you at the funeral and knew you'd come."

A knot tightened in her chest. "It's just somewhere to catch my breath."

"No, it's more than that. It was always your retreat, the place you came to find yourself. And, of course, it was the place we found each other."

"You think I've come here because of you?"

His eyes flickered over her face, his expression thoughtful. "Why not? Re-live the moments we shared here together." He looked around. "But back then it was not so sparsely furnished. What happened to the old sofa?"

She swallowed hard and tried to still the hammering of her heart as the memories came flooding back to her: of the first time he slowly undid the buttons of her dress and of the brush of his finger against her skin; of the way his hair—always too long—had tickled her breasts as his lips explored her body; of the way they'd fallen in a tangle of limbs onto the old sofa, and of the feel of him inside her.

She stood up and opened the window, closing her eyes against the cooling evening breeze, trying without success to dispel the heat her thoughts had created.

"The sofa's gone. I had to clear everything out. You know, of course, the castello was sold a year ago?"

"Sì."

"And that the year's grace the owner gave us to settle our affairs has now expired?"

"You did what you had to do to pay off your father's debts. You can make a new start for you and your sisters. You can return to England where you spent so much time with your mother's family."

"I may sound English, but I *feel* Italian. Five hundred years, Luca, half a millennium the castello has been in my family and now it's gone. I've had to let it go."

He shrugged. "Traditions are made to be broken."

She shook her head. "You'll never understand."

"No, why would I? I have no traditions, no background, as your father made clear to me." Isabella opened her mouth to speak. "You've no need to defend him." Luca shrugged. "He was right." He sighed and looked around the empty room. "But now it's all gone anyway." He swept his hand the length of the empty bookshelves that lined one of the walls between two of the four windows. "And the books have gone, too. But the shelves remain. I built them well."

The silence was filled with the memories of seven years before when Luca had worked on small building jobs around the castello and had built the shelves.

"You were always good at your work."

His hand sought out the carving on the side of the shelves. "Still here."

"You etched it in with your pen-knife: a deeply-cut heart never fades away, no matter how much work one does to eradicate the damage."

His hand instantly stopped moving and he frowned, turning slowly toward her again. "Depends on how deep the damage went. I can erase it if you'd like me to."

"Please do. The castle isn't mine any more. The new

owner is to take vacant possession tomorrow and so I'm sure he, or she, would appreciate any graffiti removed."

"Graffiti," he murmured. "Yes, I'll organize it for you."

"Not for me. For the new owner. Now, if you'll excuse me I have a meeting to attend." She began to move away but he placed a hand lightly on her arm and she stopped dead in her tracks.

"Isabella, tell me, did she suffer?"

For the first time since he'd entered the room she looked, really looked, into his eyes and saw a raw pain that cut through everything else.

She balled her hands tightly to stop them from reaching out to him and shook her head. "No, Luca, she didn't. We made sure of that." She blinked to hold back the tears that threatened. "I'm sorry. I'm so sorry."

"You were with her when she died?"

Isabella nodded.

"Good. She loved you."

Isabella gasped sharply as grief threatened to overwhelm her. "And I, her. She passed peacefully. She was just waiting to go."

"Si, si." He nodded, looking down at the ancient floor-boards, now bare of rugs. "My grandmother was a patient woman." He looked back at her again. "Unlike her grandson."

Isabella felt a smile tug at her lips.

"Yes. Unlike her grandson, who could never wait for anything."

"I waited for you."

The atmosphere changed in a heartbeat. As the sun slipped behind the mountain ridge, a dense twilight fell on them, as heavy as the shadows of the past that still haunted her.

"Not long enough, Luca."

"I gave you until the end of summer. How long did I have

to wait until you agreed to see me? Three months, three years?"

"More than one month, more than a deadline by which time if I didn't see you, you'd be gone. More than that."

"No, face it, Isabella, after your father's death you let your family persuade you I wasn't good enough. No amount of waiting would have changed that. It was that simple."

"Nothing is that simple." She shook her head, with increasing impatience, increasing fear. She could scarcely control her trembling body.

"Then what was it? Tell me. I've a right to know. You wouldn't see me, wouldn't reply to my phone calls, my emails, my letters. Why?"

The words choked her throat; her mouth was unable to form the sounds that would make him understand. She pressed her hand to her chest to try to stop the quickened breathing that threatened to balloon into a full-blown panic attack. Painful memories unfurled and lashed out at her like a poisonous snake, always waiting to bite, always hungry.

"Because I couldn't think straight."

"Thinking wasn't required. If you'd had any feelings for me you'd have come to me. But you didn't."

She stepped away from him, needing to move, needing to ground herself in the reassurance of the familiar. But there were no lamps to turn on, nothing but emptiness.

"Don't do this, Luca, not now."

"While I might be impatient, you were never good at facing things, were you Isabella? You always retreated, back into your family, back into yourself, where I could never reach you."

"Perhaps that means I don't wish to be reached."

"Perhaps." The space between them was bridged swiftly as he stepped forward and stood in front of her. He was so close that she couldn't see the whole of his face any more, just the parts: his brow drawn down as if puzzled; his eyes focusing on the individual elements of her face also, as if they were something he was only now remembering; and his lips, their tension suddenly softening.

As if in a dream he raised his hand to her hair and, so lightly she scarcely felt it, trailed the back of his finger down its sleek length. His eyes followed his finger's movement along her cheek and neck where he stopped, his fingers curling around her chin. He looked into her eyes with a depth of sadness that surprised her.

"Perhaps," he continued, "but I doubt it."

She wanted to push his hand away but was stilled by the flood of long-forgotten sensations that his touch loosed. Her gaze dropped to his mouth. She licked her lips as if her tongue wanted to explore the soft swell of his lower lip but had to be content with her own. She hoped he couldn't hear her quickened heart beat that filled her body with an urgent rhythm, compelling her to move closer to him.

"You always did think you knew me better than I knew myself."

His mouth quirked at the corners in an echo of the mischievous smile she'd known years before. "And I was right."

Before she could respond he'd dipped his head to hers and brushed her lips gently with his own. It was as if all the strength she'd spent years building had fled from her body and mind leaving only a clawing need. For an instant she shifted closer to him so their lips met once more but at the touch of his hands, running down the sides of her body, she was jolted back into awareness and pulled away.

She felt bereft—and humiliated. Within five minutes of being alone she'd made it plain that she was his for the taking. Had he come simply to do this? To show her up? To make a fool of her?

"Leave me be, Luca. I can't do this. I don't want this. You must go now. I have a meeting with my lawyer." She dragged her gaze away, walked to the door opened it and waited for him to walk through.

He looked down at the bare floor for a long moment, before he turned to her, his eyes cool now. "So you have no regrets then, Isabella?"

"Why would I have?"

"Because we loved each other once; because you turned me away because I wasn't good enough for you and your family; because you didn't tell me about our child until it was too late. No regrets for any of that?"

He didn't even sound bitter. Stated it as if he truly believed every single word.

She shook her head in confusion, unable to break through the barriers of guilt and grief and tell him the truth.

"None then. I see."

He didn't look at her as he walked out of the room. She heard his footfall on the spiral staircase, descending, moving away from her just as he had seven years before.

With one last glance around the beautiful room that had once witnessed the love affair that had changed her life, she closed the door.

Buy Now!

Made in United States
North Haven, CT
22 February 2024

49082291R00121